Family Tree Series

These stories are connected by
one woman's life spanning
from 1960 through 2010.

How did a single decision affect
her entire life, her children and
her grandchildren's futures?

Look for these new stories as the
series continues to follow Sara,
her family and her heirs.

Escape from Freedom*
Living in a Lie*
Scouting for Boys
The Legends of Lesvos
Internet Wives' Club
My Father's Seed
Heirs in Judgment
Courtship of Deceit
Harvesting the Sick
Comatose

*Published and in print

For more information:
www.redmondherring.com

Living in a Lie

Redmond Herring

authorHOUSE®

AuthorHouse™
1663 Liberty Drive
Bloomington, IN 47403

Cover design by Spoonful Productions
Photography by Spotlight Photography

Published by AuthorHouse   01/05/2015

ISBN: 978-1-4969-5259-2 (softcover)
ISBN: 978-1-4969-5258-5 (e-book)

US Copyrights
TXu1-886-535

This book is printed on acid-free paper.

First Edition

Mystery, Crime, Minnesota Author, Fiction, Redmond Herring, Investment Bankers, Red Herrings

I would like to express my sincere
thank you to my editor, Ms Red.

Redmond Herring Books
www.redmondherring.com

Living
In a
Lie

As Witnessed by Redmond Herring

Enjoy more stories in the Family Tree Series

www.redmondherring.com

Table of Contents

Chapter 1   The Venture.. 1

Chapter 2   The Capital 17

Chapter 3   Return on Investment 23

Chapter 4   Assets & Liabilities 30

Chapter 5   Cunning Confessions 67

Chapter 6   Synchronizing Life 73

Chapter 7   Unbelievable 93

Chapter 8   False Pretense 111

Chapter 9   Haunting Past.. 136

Chapter 10 Widow's Defense.................................... 140

Chapter 11 Don't Ask 150

Chapter 12 Brotherly Love 158

Chapter 13 Greed Can't Wait.................................... 163

Chapter 14 Fishing... 176

Chapter 15 The Truth Shall Set You Free 197

Chapter 16 Red Sky... 201

Chapter 17 Sailor Take Warning 220

Chapter 18 The Plan.. 235

Family Tree Series.. 238

Escape from Freedom 242

Chapter One

The Venture

IT WAS THE OLDEST ROLL-TOP desk in all of Texas. This massive manmade structure sat near the south wall on the second floor office, overlooking Ninth Avenue, in Amarillo. It was a big, brown, antique wooden piece of furniture that dominated the 'old western' office setting. The huge desk was overflowing with legal papers and positioned next to a battered wooden filing cabinet that sat in the corner of the room. Nearby was a scratched-up round oak table with four worn out barrel backed wooden chairs. Next to the desk was a faded oak high back chair with brown leather cushioning stapled on the frame with silver bottoms.

A person could only imagine the old western character that would occupy this rough domain at ten AM. As the minute hand clicked onto the hour of the antique Wells Fargo clock, the well-known character appeared in the doorway in all his glory, Attorney Andrew A. Chatsworth. A large physical man standing near six feet six inches tall was wearing a white ten-gallon cowboy hat. He looked rough and tough, not like any modern day lawyer you might see in the Potter County Court House. His face was rugged and old displaying a well trimmed white mustache.

Every detail was perfect in his appearance... silver tabs on the points of his starched white collars with his shirt pulled tight at the neck with a white string tie held together by a silver slider with a turquoise stone mounted on it. His shirt had gold monogram detailing on his chest, sleeves and cuffs. The huge silver belt buckle drew attention to his flat abdomen. This native cowboy wore starched blue jeans positioned over his authentic cowboy boots that shined like new.

"I believe we have an appointment to discuss your plans to mine some gold in these parts? Well, I'm Andrew Chatsworth... you can call me Andy for now. Is this your first time in Amarillo young man?"

"Yes, sir," answered the 30-year old executive from Minnesota. "You must think I'm crazy for traveling all this way to mine for gold. As I told you on the phone, four graduate students from West Texas A&M University recently published an article in the March issue 'Oil, Gas and Minerals' Journal, dated this year, 1980. They have engineered a new machine for extracting gold from old river beds with 80% efficiency."

The old attorney speaks…"Well, sonny, people from around the world have traveled to these parts for years searching for their fortunes in gold. Honestly, as I told you on the phone… not many prospectors have struck it rich in the past 50 years. About every 25 years or so, some crazy fool invents a new way or a better machine to get the gold out of the earth. If you have read any of the history books from around these parts, you'll find that no one has succeeded in finding any large amount of gold."

"I can help you get mineral rights and land leases if you need. I cannot help you find the gold. I cannot make any guarantees. When I get a surveyor's map of the area you want to mine, I will get the mineral rights with the needed land leases. I hope someone in your group is a surveyor and can read a map. If you do strike gold, I can protect your ass," the old council advises his guest.

"The best place to stay here in Amarillo is 'It'll Do Motel'… it's been here for years. Cheap rates, you know. After you meet up with those college wizards and if you want to go ahead with your plans, I'll help you write a LLC and a partnership agreement for you and those four engineers."

"I have reserved two white Econo cargo vans with CBs, as you requested. You will need to look at old man Haugan's warehouse to see if it will work out for you. It is big enough for two vans and some room for storage. I'll take you there when you are ready to see the building. Also, I found a furnished four-bedroom house that's for rent through August."

Living in a Lie

Darrel Emerson interrupts the lawyer and says... "Mr. Chatsworth, Andy, I appreciate all that you have done. I will take a taxi to A&M in Canyon to meet with the university students. If we all can come to terms, I will call you and then meet you back here. At that point, we can put my plans into action, pickup one of the vans, look at Haugan's building and the house and then discuss what contracts I'll need from you."

"Sir, please keep in mind that this venture is confidential and I need to trust you completely and rely on your expertise. When you have the contracts completed, I will bring the students to your office for your guidance and your insights to the local laws. I hope to keep things quiet and simple. If everything goes as planned, my expedition will be finished by September at which time I may ask you to cancel the land leases and mineral rights contracts."

As they finished their discussion, Emerson asked the lawyer to call a taxi that could take him to the university five miles south to Canyon. The men shook hands and parted as the cab appeared by the building's main entrance. The trip would be a half-hour ride south to West Texas A&M Campus where Emerson would meet his new partners in the main lobby of the Science & Engineering Building. The four graduate students were on time as was Emerson. It was high noon. Even though it was springtime, the air was already sweltering hot in Texas.

I introduced myself and they did, as well. "Hi, my name is "Tyler Castor." "Hi, my name is Sally Livingston." "Hi, my name is Brook Madison." "Hi, my name is Sam Wade."

Sam speaks first... "Sir, we would like to thank you for coming here to meet with us and to see our invention. Did you have any problems finding us? As the token male in this cadre, I am expected to do most of the talking. I cannot quite understand why. We all know women talk more than men but I'm ok with it."

Emerson speaks, "You can all call me Darrel. I'm not your superior. I hope that we will be equal partners after we discuss all the details. When are you finished here at the university?"

Sam replies, "We can be out of here first thing Wednesday morning. Let's go look at our new invention in the lab and review our documentation from a recent experiment."

They spend over an hour reviewing every aspect of their new gold extracting machine examining all the functions and the 'whistle and bells' for operating the apparatus. It actually worked in the laboratory. However, how will it work in an arroyo? Of course, there were many questions and many problems to be resolved with many unknown circumstances to overcome.

Emerson was satisfied and interested in starting "in the field" experiments and forming a partnership with the four graduates. He explained to the novice inventors..."We will form a LLC to start our business and a limited partnership contract will document our ownership of the patents filed for your invention." Emerson agreed to pay all legal costs, filing fees, land leases, living expenses, equipment, supplies and administrative fees. At the end of August, the four students would be paid $2,500 each as a bonus for completing their experiments. The partners would share equally

Living in a Lie

in all royalties, user's fees and gold revenues. He suggested to the group, "In order to simplify all communications, let's call your invention 'Red Rover' instead of the gold extracting machine."

Darrel then outlined his plans, "You four will conduct the needed experiments, documentation of your findings and examination of your soil samplings, Monday through Friday. On Saturdays, you'll do maintenance on all the trucks and equipment. Sundays will be personal time for grocery shopping, laundry and rest."

Darrel went on to explain, "I will be traveling back and forth to Bloomington, Minnesota to conduct business and oversee my marketing plans. With my experience and connections, I will secure capital to fund our expedition and possibly for future developments. One of you will need to be the project manager and responsible for taking pictures, writing summaries and documenting expenses."

Everyone was excited to get underway with the project and agreed to all the terms Emerson proposed... "The Red Rover Limited Liability Contract will be ready to sign on Wednesday and the students could move from their campus dorm to a furnished four-bedroom house in Amarillo. On Thursday, the team of engineers could purchase all necessary equipment and supplies including a new desktop computer and a 35mm camera. On Friday, we'll organize the warehouse site and build sifting tables and examination stations."

"You will have to get a written release from the university to remove Red Rover on Wednesday. I'll have a van with ramps so we can take Red Rover to the warehouse for safekeeping. I'll have a second van for moving your personal effects out of your dorm and into the house. If you have any personal vehicles, you can store them in the warehouse until September. Monday will be our first day in the field. I have located a number of potential mining sites along the old Red River bed. We need to survey these sites and complete all plot maps in order for our attorney to get mineral rights and land leases. We will not use Red Rover until all the legalities are final. However, as you can anticipate, there is a lot to get done before we begin our mining experiments."

Darrel continued... "I'm sure you'll have many questions and concerns. We can discuss your ideas and develop our plans at our evening dinners. I expect you to stay together as a team with no outside friendships or relationships. Friday nights we'll have a big dinner together and Saturday nights we'll go out to the local night spots for hamburgers and beer, as a team."

"Are you all in? Ok, I'll be back here at eight AM on Wednesday. Thank you."

Emerson called his lawyer before leaving the university to instruct him to begin the paper work. "I'll be back in Amarillo by four PM to pickup one of the cargo vans and then check into the motel. Tomorrow morning at nine AM, I'll pick you up at your office and review the warehouse and the rental house. I'll give you more details when we are together."

After working at an investment bank in Minnesota for the past ten years, Darrel Emerson was now a self-employed owner of a

Living in a Lie

gold mining operation in Texas. He was investing his life savings of $50,000 on the startup venture with no prior experience in precious metals, mining or managing a partnership. Darrel had drafted his business plan a year ago waiting for the right opportunity to start up his own venture capital investment firm and knowing the right people would help his business succeed.

Once the Red Rover Project had the mineral rights, land leases and a viable business with pending patents, Emerson could start contacting potential investors. When his team of mining engineers develop their photographs of the Red Rover, printed copies of their certified surveys showing the mining sites and then print a written prospectus detailing the entire operation, Emerson could make plans for raising capital. Meanwhile, he would begin his marketing campaign by sending custom invitations to his list of wealthy prospects announcing the Red Rover Project. In that initial mailing, he would include a letter, business card and RSVP for the investor to return to Darrel if they were interested in receiving a prospectus detailing the venture.

Most investment banks had never used this creative approach but Emerson knew from his experience, investors like to be 'teased a little' before committing any money. It was like 'being invited to a private party' for a select group of people. The returned RSVP cards would give Darrel permission to mail his prospectus to a very elite crowd of prospective investors. The invitations, RSVP cards and the envelopes would be printed on the highest quality of linen paper with a beautiful gold embossed logo and gold engraved copy. 'Top shelf, classy and expensive.'

Emerson was betting everything he owned on this venture... The Red Rover Project. All the years of working in the investment and banking business were on the line. He would either 'go broke' or have enough capital to start his new investment firm called Redstone Venture Capital, LLC.

Much like the investment opportunity he offered, this venture would be 'high-risk' with great possibilities for huge returns. Darrel Emerson had an old adage hanging in his Bloomington office... 'A turtle never gets ahead until it sticks its neck out.' This was the opportunity for Darrel to become 'one of the big guys' at the country club and a wealthy man.

Was it worth it?

Emerson's initial investment would be used up at a rate of $10,000 per month just to make the Red Rover Project feasible. He needed investment capital by August to payoff his debts in order to survive in September, when he could possibly lose his office and his home, if Red Rover did not generate a return.

In the next few days, he would pay all expenses with Red Rover business checks drawing funds from three different bank accounts in Texas, Minnesota and Nevada. There would be no turning back. Even though he had deposits in all three banks, he worried there might be some unexpected problem that might delay his plans. He worried about Chatsworth getting the mineral rights and land leases. In addition, the worst thing that could happen would be the Red Rover machine not working as anticipated.

Could Darrel Emerson convince the 'high roller' crowd to invest in his venture? The price of gold was down to $450 an ounce with prime interest rate up to 15%. Were his college professors' theories accurate? "Gold is a good investment when interest rates are high."

On his flight out of Amarillo, Darrel was able to reflect on the events of the past ten days in setting up the Red Rover Project. He was confident his team of young engineers would do their job to prove Red Rover's usefulness. He was certain that attorney Chatsworth was competent and thorough in managing all the legalities of the expedition. The next two weeks were critical in developing the needed prospectus.

Upon his arrival in Minnesota, Darrel instructed his printer to move ahead with typesetting and keylining Redstone's first marketing campaign. He would approve the artwork ASAP to expedite production of the invitation package. Mailing labels needed to be typeset with Emerson's confidential list of prospective investors. To avoid mistakes each step of the printing process was carefully monitored.

Each evening, Darrel called his team in Texas to get an update of the mining operation, the photography results and the documentation for the prospectus. Everything was going as planned. Chatsworth had secured certificates for the mineral rights, land leases and pending patents.

All Darrel Emerson needed was an influx of capital from interested investors to pay expenses, expedition costs and development costs. Chatsworth needed to create stock certificates, a corporate logbook and a separate bank account.

The team of engineers needed to keep surveying and mining the sands of the old Red River bed. Each week they would move to another site farther south, down river. Each week they would continue sifting through the red sand looking for particles of gold.

Now the big question remained unanswered... "Is there gold in those dried up creek beds?"

Andy Chatsworth, the old wise attorney, had witnessed many anxious people come to Texas in search of gold. After living in Amarillo for over 60 years, Chatsworth watched prospectors come and go without finding gold. Speculators coming from everywhere to go home broke. The young entrepreneur from Minnesota would not find gold either. Why would anyone in his right mind search for gold when the price of an ounce was going down and there was no gold to be found in Texas?

So what was Darrel Emerson up to? He was spending a lot of cash on a hunch. However, the important thing was Emerson was paying for everything up front. Chatsworth's bill was always paid in full. Was Emerson going to steal the graduate students' invention and sell it without sharing the royalties with the young engineers?

Chatsworth could not see the big picture yet. However, he was watching the 'Northern Boy' very closely. Things did not add up in the old lawyer's mind.

Living in a Lie

As summer heated up the Texas desert, the four graduate engineers started grumbling to each other about the lousy thankless job they accepted.

First, Brook Madison began complaining about their working conditions out in the arroyos that were hot, dry and filthy. Almost daily, the winds would pickup the red sand swirling it into dust storms that blew through their excavation site causing them to take cover in the Econo Van.

Brook finally said her piece to her peers, "Why in the hell are we out here? I never imagined having such a shitty job after spending four years in college. I would rather be waiting on tables in a crummy bar in Dallas, At least then I could go home to my parent's house to shower and sleep in my own bedroom. I could be driving a new car and dating. Who is this Emerson guy telling us we can't have friends here in Amarillo?"

Sally Livingston joined in, "I agree, if it weren't for $2,500 bonus at the end of August, I would have gone home to Houston. Sure, Emerson is paying for all of our living expenses. I figured it out last night; we are making $625 per week. That calculates out to be $89 per day, seven days a week. It amounts to $11 per hour."

Sam Wade was sympathetic to their discomforts but encouraged them to look at the big picture. "Hey, I agree with your dissatisfaction with the terms of our employment and our living conditions. However, if the Red Rover proves out to be a great invention, we'll all be rich when Emerson sells our invention to mining companies all over the world."

Sam interjected, "We'll become famous engineers for inventing the gold extracting machine. Gold mining companies will offer us big salaries to train others and to build newer and better machines. All of us want our names written up in the 'Oil, Gas and Minerals' Journal. Isn't this what we all want in the beginning of our professional careers?"

Tyler Castor, their team leader, agreed with the others but encouraged them to believe in what they were doing.

"Hey guys, remember the poster on our professor's classroom wall. 'A turtle will NOT get ahead without sticking its neck out.' We are all inexperienced in business, unknown in our field without having real jobs as engineers. We can endure these few hardships now and add this internship experience to our resumes. Emerson indicated that he would give us letters of recommendation and professional affidavits for our engineering accomplishments. These four months will be 'money in the bank' giving us creditability for the rest of our lives."

Tyler added more words of support to her team, "We are halfway through the summer with only eight weeks to go. We can finish this project as promised and be proud of what we have accomplished. Before any of us accepted Emerson's opportunity, our futures were uncertain. None of us had plans for the summer. And the greatest benefit is we have become close friends, a bond the will last a lifetime."

Living in a Lie

"Hello, who's calling?" the voice on the telephone in Amarillo questioned the caller. Tyler Castor had answered the phone while working on the computer that afternoon.

"Tyler, its Darrel Emerson. How are things going?"

"Everything is fine, Darrel. The others are at the warehouse and I'm working on the prospectus. It's almost finished. Hey, we really have some great photos to show you. Red Rover is working fine. We've had some concerns with all the weight on the front tires when extracting the sand but Sam was able to block up the frame with 2x4s... keeping the load off of the wheels."

"How much gold have you found?" Emerson inquired.

"We have about two ounces. I bagged it, logged it in the journal and photographed the nuggets. We thought you would like to see them before we take the cache to Chatsworth for safekeeping."

"Great... Tyler, it sounds as if you are managing the project well. How are the others getting along? Are they ok with you being the leader? Any attitude problems?"

"Everyone is doing fine... you were correct in having us get off the mining site before noon. It really gets hot out there in the afternoon."

"Tyler, will I be able to edit the prospectus soon? I'll be down there on Monday. Can you have most of it ready?"

Tyler answers Darrel's last question, "Yes, it'll be ready. Wait until you see the photo we picked for the front cover. The morning sun is shinning over the hills, softly lighting the red sand in the creek bed, giving off an awesome reddish glow with vivid blue skies in the background. The camera we bought is wonderful."

"Ok, say hi to the others and let them know I'll be arriving at the house around four PM on Monday. Hey, lets all of us go out for a big dinner in the evening. We all have a lot to talk about." Emerson hangs up and checks his airplane tickets.

Emerson was able to leave his office early that Friday afternoon knowing that the printer completed the first mailing of the Invitation. The first mailing was 250 pieces and if a second mailing was necessary, another 250 pieces were ready to mail. During the next week, he expected the RSVPs to begin arriving in his Bloomington PO Box.

The next stage would include design and layout of the prospectus, color separations of the 35mm photos, film preparation for the 4/color lithographic plates and then 4/color offset printing on a Heidelberg press. If everything went as planned, the printer would be mailing the 4/color prospectus including an inserted cover letter by July 1.

Emerson's plans were right on schedule. He would spend the first couple of weeks in July calling on prospective investors from his Bloomington office and he needed to hire an administrative assistant. He called his Minnesota attorney and instructed him to register his limited liability corporation in the State of Nevada.

Darrel celebrated his progress by taking his wife to Eddy Webster's for dinner that Saturday night. She hardly knew anything

Living in a Lie

about Darrel's business dealings and he wanted to keep her informed to what was going on. She voiced her concerns about the possibility of losing their home but was appeased when her husband reviewed his meticulous business plans.

"The risks are worth the rewards," Darrel reassured his wife of ten years. "By September, Redstone Venture Capital will be worth more than one million dollars after our initial investment of $50,000 is repaid to us."

Chapter Two

The Capital

ALL HIS PLANNING AND ATTENTION to the details combined with his experience and connections made Darrel Emerson a millionaire with his initial stock offer. The Red Rover Project was a hit with investors who were eager to embrace new and innovative ideas. Emerson's professional prospectus was well designed and beautifully printed, using dramatic photos, precise charts and graphs showing results of the field experiments and written documents indicating favorable results for extracting gold from abandoned creek beds.

Profiling the four graduate engineers and their research at West Texas A&M University gave creditability to the venture. Their new extraction processes and their new invention were exclusive to Emerson's mining operation. 'Drilling down under surface sands in abandoned creek beds, near known mineral deposits and gold veins, deep enough to get below years of surface erosion, stir up the sand and mineral deposits and then vacuum the fine particles into bags on the surface. Empty the bags into large vibrating sifter screens while picking out the gold nuggets and particles.' Voila !

Earlier prospectors had discovered and excavated gold in the same area for nearly 50 years in the eighteenth century. However, most of the mineral deposits were uncovered and excavated ending all future strip mining operations. Red Rover was the solution for the next logical process. Without this invention, prospectors could not dig deep enough to excavate underneath the reddish surface sands of the dried up creek beds, which had been covered with centuries of blowing desert sands.

The students' theory was simply common sense. The earlier processes of extracting gold from strip mining massive amounts of sand, was less than 20% efficient. Technology was not available to improve the process. So what happened to the remaining 80% of the excavated gold?

The answer... the missed gold particles simply washed downstream sinking into eroded channels at the bottom of creek beds. Gold is heavier than sand and therefore settles below it.

Along comes Red Rover to suck it out of the forgotten creeks.

The young engineers were proving their theories and testing their extracting machine in the Red River Valley of Northern Texas expecting to reclaim the lost minerals from years past.

Over 100 investors besieged Redstone Venture Capital wanting to buy stock in Emerson's Red Rover Project. Only a limited number of investors could buy in and only sophisticated investors, those who had personal assets of at least $10,000,000. The investment trust was a 'UIT', legally known as 'unit investment trust'. A UIT typically will make a one-time 'public offering' with only a specific, fixed number of units. Investors could review all the details of the Red Rover Project prospectus portfolio held by the UIT.

Darrel was the sole owner and stockholder of Redstone Venture Capital, LLC, which was a registered limited liability corporation in the State of Nevada. He had no other partners. All expenses, losses and profits were controlled by Darrel Emerson.

Redstone was the sponsor and broker for the Red Rover Project.

In order to buy shares, investors were required to purchase a minimum of 100,000 shares at $10 per share, or a total investment of $1,000,000. Redstone charged 1% as a Registration Fee along with 5% for a Purchase Fee. That is, the price the investor pays to purchase the UIT shares is an approximate cost per share of NAV, less any fees that the fund imposes at the purchase. The share price of a traditional UIT is based on their NAV (Net Assets Value).

Redstone's upfront costs were $50,000, so therefore one share was valued at $9.40 when purchased. The prospectus informed investors that there was an early redemption fee of 2% per share of the NAV, as well.

Darrel Emerson's Redstone Venture Capital, LLC sold 2,500,000 shares of the Red Rover Project, (25 Investors paid a total of $25,000,000) netting Emerson $1,500,000 in upfront fees...which was perfectly legal.

Darrel Emerson became a millionaire on August 31, 1980. Not bad for putting together a gold mining venture with his start up capital of $50,000.

On August 30, Darrel met with his team of engineers at the warehouse in Amarillo to close the experimental mining operation. The two leased vans should be returned in the morning and the mining and survey equipment should be resold to the army surplus store today. Emerson would pay for storing Red Rover in a secure rental locker for the next year.

Emerson reviewed the project, "You all did a great job in accomplishing what we set out to do. Red Rover worked as you predicted. Our four month operation uncovered ten ounces of gold, which is worth $480 per ounce totaling $4,800. I have a check for each of you of $960, I get one-fifth, as well."

The businessman continued, "Each of you must sign these documents agreeing to close our partnership. We all still own shares in Red Rover and if the extracting machine is sold, each of you will receive one-fifth of the sale. I agreed to pay each of you $2,500 at the end of August. However, the project proved to be more valuable than I anticipated. So, therefore, I'm adding $500 to your bonuses. Here is another check for each of you for $3,000."

Emerson concluded his instructions, "We all need to be out of the house by noon tomorrow. I have a cleaning crew that will tidy up before I return the keys to the owner. Please keep in touch over the next 12 months and if you need a reference in your future, please do contact me. Tyler... if you are interested, I might have a job for you in my Las Vegas office. It would be great if we all celebrated tonight at dinner. I'll buy."

The engineers were pleased with their final reward as Emerson left the building and drove over to meet with his lawyer, Andrew A. Chatsworth. All their legal matters were final so Emerson paid Chatsworth's final invoice and thanked him for his service.

"Please call me if you have problems or concerns. I'll be leaving town on Sunday," Darrel instructed the lawyer. "Even though we did not find a large amount of gold, the mining expedition proved to be successful."

Chatsworth never found out what the 'Northern Boy' was doing in Texas. Emerson did not find much gold. What he did reclaim hardly paid for a week's worth of expenses.

"Another speculator gone bust" the old Texas lawyer told others.

That evening the team reviewed their assessment of Red Rover with Emerson. "The experiments did prove Red Rover's extracting value but the machine should be put in moth balls until the price of gold goes up. Then it would become more valuable."

Sam Wade decided to return to A&M and get his Masters. Brook Madison had plans to go to RIT for her Masters. Sally Livingston would be returning home to live with her parents near Houston for a year. Tyler Castor was interested in Emerson's job opportunity in Las Vegas. They would talk more on Saturday.

A job well done.

Chapter Three

Return on Investment

TYLER CASTOR SAID HER GOODBYE'S to her fellow engineers as they left the rented house and headed out of town to their personal destinations. She had packed up her 1980 Mazda and waited until Darrel Emerson finished his business with the property owner. Tyler wanted to know all the details of Darrel's job opportunity in Las Vegas. It was getting late in the afternoon and she was getting hungry and wanted Darrel's undivided attention.

Tyler was a beautiful woman with an athletic figure with long blonde hair, a fresh young complexion, blue eyes with long eyelashes and an everlasting smile. She was five feet seven inches tall, one hundred twenty pounds and enjoyed wearing tight jeans with halter tops. Her father, a well-known surgeon in Oklahoma City, had pampered and spoiled his 24-year-old daughter with expensive gifts and a lavish lifestyle. Her clothes were the best money could buy. Upon graduating from a private high school, her close friends tried to encourage her to become a fashion model in New York City.

She was intelligent, well-spoken and carried herself with grace and confidence. She was anxious to start her new career wherever the best opportunity might be for her to succeed on her terms, with her abilities and with her knowledge. She was hoping that Darrel could offer her more than just a job. She wanted a career that promised her fame, fortune and independence.

The Red Rover Project was boring for her and a waste of her time. However, she endured the uncomfortable life and the dirty environment to prove her abilities to Darrel Emerson.

Finally, Darrel was ready to go as he entered Tyler's sports car and thanked her for her patience and for giving him a ride to the Best Western Hotel near the airport. He suggested they eat lunch in the hotel restaurant and discuss the job opportunity he had for the graduate.

The afternoon temperature was near one hundred degrees without any breeze. The hotel swimming pool looked refreshing but the couple had business to discuss before Emerson could relax and cool off. He knew Tyler was in a hurry to begin her three hour drive home to Oklahoma City but the cunning executive had other plans. He would take advantage of her sanguinity and purposely delay her from leaving Amarillo that afternoon. He had the 'carrot of opportunity' for the young woman and lots of money to entice her to come to work for him in Las Vegas.

"Well, Tyler, let me tell you about my expansion plans in Nevada and how you can be part of my business. You did such a great job in managing the Red Rover Project and creating that outstanding prospectus, I can utilize your talents in many ways. In reviewing your college curriculum, I see you had minors in business economics and in graphic design. As a graduate engineer, you can be of tremendous benefit in my future business ventures into oil, gas and precious metals," the venture capitalist explained.

"I can pay you a good salary with great benefits and you will travel throughout North America presenting investment opportunities to the 'Country Club Crowd'. You will stay in the best hotels, drive the finest rental cars and have an expensive clothing allowance," Darrel continued making his pitch to the mature young woman.

The university graduate responded, "Darrel, please understand, I'm not interested in becoming a field engineer or supervisor ever again. I took part in the Red Rover Project to prove myself to you. I expect only the best in my future endeavors... nothing less than the 'Country Club Crowd.' Can you afford me?"

Tyler continued her negotiations..."I'll need a salary of $1,000 per week, medical insurance and car allowance, paid tuition for evening classes in computer technology, two weeks of paid vacation and the promise of partnership within two years."

Emerson hesitated before answering, "I'll agree to those terms...how about I get you a room here for the night. We have a lot to discuss and I really need to cool off in the hotel swimming pool and relax. Do you have a swim suit?"

The young woman replies, "Yes, I do have a suit with me. I was on my high school swim team. I love swimming. I guess I will stay the night and drive home in the morning. However, you do not need to get another room. I can stay in your room. If that's okay with you?"

Darrel Emerson was hoping she would catch on to his subtle hints and stay the night. If she felt the same attraction as he did, the night would be unforgettable. First, he knew they would play a game of innuendos while bathing in the swimming pool. Tyler had been flirting with him all the time they were in the restaurant.

"Tyler, let's get your suitcase and go to our room. I need to cool off and get in the pool."

Emerson went into the motel room bathroom first to change into his swimsuit. When he came out, the voluptuous young woman was in her underwear looking for her swimsuit in her suitcase.

"Darrel, you go on ahead I'll join in you in a few minutes."

When Tyler entered the doorway to the indoor swimming pool, she looked like a goddess from Neptune as her long blonde hair fluttered in the slight breeze. As she strutted towards the pool on the runway of ceramic tiles, every fashion photographer in New York would envy the opportunity to capture her breath-taking beauty.

The 'Minnesota nice guy' became embarrassed as his swimsuit stretched outward because of his underwater erection. Emerson took a deep breath as he admired the beautiful college girl as she entered the auditorium in her bikini swimsuit. Her nicely toned athletic body looked like a model out of a Playboy Magazine. After she entered the water, she swam over to Darrel and gave him a huge French kiss. At that point, they both anticipated the lustful evening to come. Tyler rubbed him intimately without hesitation.

Their amorous play began as she swam away teasing him and encouraging Darrel to catch her. She was a better swimmer and laughed when he could not keep up. He was determined but could not catch the expert swimmer so he stopped and began taunting her. Tyler gave in, plunged under the water from the opposite end of the pool and swam the entire distance to resurface next to him as she rubbed his groin when coming up for air.

The young woman had taken control and then kissed him again, "Darrel, I know what you did with the Red Rover Project. You might have fooled Chatsworth and the other engineers. However, I know how you leveraged the mining expedition and Red Rover by selling limited shares to wealthy investors under the disguise of a UIT. Remember, I just finished my minor in business finance. I know what venture capitalists do. You sold shares in a bogus gold mining business. I wrote the prospectus. So I know. How much did you make on fees and commissions?"

"Tyler, I've come to appreciate your many talents and business instincts. You will become my most valued investment. Are you interested in joining my venture capital business in Nevada?"

"Darrel, now that you respect my intelligence and appreciate my virtues, I'll need more incentives and rewards added onto your previous offer. I can only anticipate that I will become your mistress at night and a very valuable partner during the day. I want the business to buy me a condominium in Las Vegas, a new BMW and I'll want a written partnership agreement stating the terms of my employment."

"Well, Tyler, let's go upstairs and spend the night working out all the details. I'll order up some champagne to celebrate our consolidation and partnership." With that statement, Darrel Emerson advanced his second scheme of the year.

"I look forward to working with you and pleasing you in so many ways," Ms. Tyler Castor conceded and was eager to begin her new career.

———

Darrel Emerson arrived at the Minneapolis/St Paul Airport near six o'clock on Sunday evening, picked up his luggage, called his wife and then found his Lincoln Continental Mark IV in the parking ramp. He was happy to return home to sleep in his own bed with his gorgeous wife who was delighted to hear all the good news about the Red Rover Project and Redstone's Portfolio of investors. She was especially relieved to know that their initial investment of $50,000 was back in their joint bank account. They would be able to keep their house, their new cars and their savings.

The next couple of weeks would be stressful for Darrel as he planned the next stage of the Red Rover Project. He would be meeting with Tyler in ten days to get her setup in Las Vegas and begin preparing her for his next venture. He had a lot on his mind and fell asleep soon after his wife exercised her amorous marital rights.

Chapter Four

Assets & Liabilities

TYLER WAS WAITING IN HER new BMW for Darrel's arrival from Minnesota that warm September afternoon. His non-stop flight to Las Vegas was due to arrive at two o'clock as the desert heat created swirling mirages on the tarmac runways at McCarran International.

The young college graduate was anxious to see her recent admirer and employer who had offered her a dream job in investment banking a couple of weeks ago. Last week she had received an advancement of $2,000 along with Emerson's employment contract mailed to her new living address at Redstone Venture Capital's condominium in Spring Valley. The advancement would cover her expenses until she was on the company payroll.

Tyler had mixed emotions as she greeted her boss with a hug and kiss curbside near the passenger pickup area. He seemed happy to see her as he handed her a bouquet of red roses. As they drove away from the airport, Ms. Castor confronted Emerson.

"I'm really disappointed with your misleading employment proposition for working together here in Vegas. When we were in Texas, I clearly stipulated that I wanted to become a partner not an employee. I wanted the business, Redstone, to purchase a condo in my name. I want the BMW in my name, not in your name."

"Darrel, I'm not a naive college blonde who might have been a football cheerleader. I understand business law, corporate taxes, the benefits of stock ownership and I know how your marital assets held jointly with your wife can affect my assets. If you ever get a divorce, your dissolution will not impinge on my life."

In Emerson's anticipation to be with his new mistress, her anguish had destroyed his excitement. He needed solace, comfort; not discontent and criticism. He had fantasies of having an evening of endless sex with his new attractive investment. However, her anger dissipated his testosterone.

"Tyler, let's relax and enjoy each other tonight. I need to shower and change clothes before dinner. I want to have a nice romantic dinner at the Grand Hotel and then drinks in the swimming pool before satisfying our sexual needs. We can resolve all your concerns at the office tomorrow. Let's leave business in the office. Okay?"

Darrel Emerson had remembered the old golden rule early on in his investment career... 'The one who holds the gold makes the rules.' He was not about to let this inexperienced, presumptuous, narcissistic and conceited bitch tell him how to control his gold. He would use her talents and her intrinsic value while satisfying his personal sexual desires. No woman will ever control his hard earned wealth! Especially when they begin to think they are essential to his success.

Darrel knew exactly how to outwit this Phoenix.

Over the next four weeks, Darrel and Tyler rewrote their agreements, purchased a new condo for Tyler and remodeled Redstone's new corporate offices. Darrel had cooked up his next investment scheme together with his new limited partner. Every evening they enjoyed dinner, swimming and corporal activities. During office hours, these eager schemers functioned as a well oiled slot machine creating a colossal investment scheme that would triumph any Wall Street IPO.

Red Rover offered investors a diverse stock option plan called a Hedge Fund where their initial investment dollars, i.e. stock in The Red Rover Project, would be leveraged to buy into a new type of REIT, a Real Estate Investment Trust fund. REIT's were a new security product on the market that sold like stocks, invested in real estate directly, either through properties or through mortgages.

Redstone Investments created this speculative portfolio under the name of Red Earth Properties, LLC registered in Nevada.

The investors would receive special tax considerations typically offered to high rollers who needed high returns, as well as liquidity in their investments.

Redstone was one of the first investment firms to offer Equity REITs, Mortgage REITs and Hybrid REITs. Big institutional investors such as pension funds, insurance companies and mutual funds were all interested in Redstone's avant-garde portfolio.

Emerson, along with his protégé, created one of the newest investment funds in real estate development and eventually their firm would create REITs for oil and gas exploration.

In order to accommodate new investors, the venture capital investment company had to hire dozens of employees in their headquarters while adding satellite offices in Dallas, Chicago, Miami, Minneapolis and New York.

Within ten months, Emerson's life changed beyond his wildest dreams. He became one of the 'movers and shakers' in the country club crowd and personally invested millions in his own real estate properties in Las Vegas, Cabos San Lucas and in Minnesota. His original investment firm, Redstone Venture Capital, LLC, had an investment portfolio worth over fifty million dollars.

Darrel Emerson, a poor farm boy from Waterville, Minnesota became a wealthy venture capitalist with a personal net worth of over ten million dollars, 10 years after graduating from Mankato State College.

Tyler Castor was Vice President of Operations managing their corporate staff while overseeing all investment portfolios. To attract more investors Tyler presented their firm's Portfolio of Investments at major country clubs throughout North America where wealthy and famous investors spend time.

As a very attractive, sophisticated, knowledgeable broker, she traveled to private clubs socializing with prospective investors. Her status attracted a lot of attention, as she became a well-known expert in REIT funds. Her professional book of contacts and investors would rival any 'Who's Who Directory' on Wall Street.

It was not long before major investment firms noticed her and tried recruiting her but to no avail. Tyler was a master partner in a private partnership that secured her future with Darrel Emerson. No one could fracture her position, not even Darrel who held 70% of the controlling shares in a private holding company called Redhead Investments, LLC registered in the Cayman Islands.

Darrel Emerson knew in his gut that he needed to shelter his personal finances before anyone, including the IRS, could consider seizing his collective assets so he began seeking a private professional counselor. A well-known investment tycoon who lived in Minnesota suggested a professional confidant by the name of Redmond Herring.

"Herring is confidential and can be trusted as a secret executor for your offshore bank accounts. Tell no one... not even your wife or any partners. Keep it confidential."

Emerson met with me, privately, at the Decathlon Club in Bloomington, Minnesota on May 23, 1981 to establish our top secret partnership. Emerson agreed to pay me, in cash, an annual retainer of $25,000.

I agreed to meet with Emerson privately whenever he might call to review the covert accounts. "No paper records to leave a trail of evidence," I reassured him.

"Say, Redmond, are you interested in doing some clandestine work for me? I need to circumvent a potential problem that could hurt me in the future. Okay, listen carefully..."

The illicit partners completed their transactions and left separately agreeing to meet in Las Vegas on July 3 at the Cosmopolitan. I anticipated having all the secret Cayman Islands bank accounts ready for deposit and safekeeping.

Emerson's other concerns would be dealt with as well.

―――――――――

"Tyler Castor, is that you. It's Sam Wade from A&M University in Amarillo. Remember me?" the voice on Tyler's home phone inquired.

"Yes, it's me and how are you, Sam?" Tyler replied.

Sam responded, "I'm okay. Remember Brook Madison? She went onto RIT after leaving Amarillo. She was with us on the Red Rover Project."

"Yes, I remember her. She was really a smart girl... especially in engineering, gas and oil explorations and... Patent Rights, Copyrights and US Inventions," Tyler answered.

"She was working on her dissertation for her Masters, 'Protecting Inventions with Patent Rights,' when she called me to share her discovery. I was not home when she called. She left a message and told me to call her ASAP. I was gone for the weekend fossil hunting in the desert. I finally retrieved her message from my voice-recording machine Monday morning. When I called her, her roommate answered the phone. I was shocked to learn that a car near the campus hit Brook on Sunday evening. She was walking home from her job at the bookstore. She's dead!" Sam explained with concern.

"What? You've got to be kidding me," Tyler responded.

"It's a fact. Her parents are flying her body home to Dallas for funeral arrangements this week. The viewing and funeral will be at ten AM on Friday at Gibson's Funeral Home in Arlington. I'll be there... can you? I've called Sally Livingston. She'll be there."

"Wow, I'm in shock. Yes, I'll be there for sure. I'll drive down on Thursday and stay at the Sheraton in Arlington. Thanks for calling. See you then," Tyler closed their conversation.

Sam's call left many questions in Tyler's mind. What information did Brook want to share with Sam? How could a car hit her if she was walking home on campus? Aren't there sidewalks for students? Did the police find the hit and run driver? Did Brook share any information with her roommate before making that mysterious call to Sam?

Tyler's mind was in overdrive with many unanswered questions hoping Brook's parents could shed some light on this unfortunate accident.

The next day Tyler called Darrel Emerson who was working in his Minneapolis office and informed him that she needed to take some time off for Brook's funeral.

"Do you want to meet me in Dallas and pay your respects to Brook's family?" Tyler asked Darrel.

"Tyler, I would like to but I can't. My wife has planned a special birthday party for our daughter who is turning ten on Thursday. Please have flowers sent to the funeral home and give my condolences to her family," Darrel responded.

"I'll be returning to Vegas next Sunday night so could you pick me up at the airport around seven o'clock?" Emerson asked his partner.

"Darrel, I'm going to take some time to visit with my friends from A&M and then drive to Oklahoma City to see my family for maybe a week. It's been a busy year and I need a vacation. I'll be back in Vegas the following weekend. I'll call to let you know when I'll arrive at my condo," Tyler answered.

Brook's parents did not spare any expense for their only daughter's funeral and reception. Hundreds of friends and relatives attended the ceremony at the family's Methodist Church and the entire assembly drove in the motorcade to the cemetery. Brook was well liked and respected by everyone. Her parents invited and paid the expenses for Brook's RIT friends including her roommate to fly to Texas for the funeral.

The Dallas Newspaper highlighted Brook Madison's tragic accident primarily because her father was a well-known successful businessperson and a State Senator. John Madison was putting a lot of pressure on the Rochester Police Department in hopes of finding his daughter's killer. No one had come forward and no one saw the accident.

RIT held a prayer vigil that Friday evening in Brook's memory.

Saturday morning Tyler Castor invited her past classmates from A&M and Brook's RIT classmates to spend breakfast together in remembrance of Brook. It was at that time Tyler questioned Brook's roommate, Colleen Williams, about Brook's call to Sam Wade a week ago.

Colleen presented her information with caution and care to the table of curious listeners. "It was in May when Brook began acting unusual. She seemed angry and upset for days. When I asked 'what was her problem?' She said that she had been in contact with the US Patent office and discovered an error in their records. The Washington Bureaucrats insisted their records were correct and her assertions were incorrect. She told me she was really pissed off. The summer after graduating from A&M she worked her ass off in the Texas desert for some businessman from Minnesota who had promised her and her friends an equal ownership in an invention they had built. The patent office had no documentation with the student's name recorded with any invention."

"Wait a minute," Tyler insisted. "That was our group, Sam, Sally, Brook and me."

"Are you saying that Brook discovered that our names were not listed as the patent holders for our gold extracting machine?" Sam inquired. "Whose name is registered as the patent holder?"

"The businessman from Minnesota used a trade name 'Red Rover' which was copyrighted by Darrel Emerson," the RIT student explained.

"Whoa," Sally Livingston cried out. "That swindling bastard. He promised us equal ownership in our invention that we designed, we built and we tested all summer in that god forsaken river bed and then he screwed us out of any future royalties."

Sam looked directly at Tyler and asked, "Tyler, isn't Emerson the guy you went to work for in Las Vegas last September? You told me you were in a partnership with him. Has he moved Red Rover out of Amarillo? Has he sold it to anyone? Tyler what's going on?"

"I do not know. Darrel has not mentioned anything about Red Rover or the pending patents," the co-ed responded to the pressing inquiry. "Matter of fact, there was nothing mentioned when he closed the investment portfolio last fall. I should have asked but I did not."

"Well it seems that Brook wanted to share her discovery with Sam when she called him," Sally inserted her thoughts into the conversation. "It really is suspicious that she died before disclosing her findings to any of us. We should share this information with Mr. Madison so he can alert the authorities in New York. Sam, do you know where our invention is stored? Is it in Amarillo? Do you think that old lawyer Chatsworth knows anything about this?"

"I'll have to check things out when I return to A&M," Sam responded.

Tyler speaks up, "Sam, I think I'll drive up to Amarillo tomorrow so we can question Chatsworth together on Monday. He'll know where the Red Rover is stored and I want copies of the patent registrations and our partnership agreements."

"Okay, Tyler, I'll be heading back today," Sam concedes.

After breakfast, everyone offered their farewell greetings promising to stay in touch with Tyler as she volunteered to take the lead in the investigation. Sally really seemed distraught and upset with the thoughts of missing any royalties that their college invention might render. Sam was perplexed with the whole situation but willing to help in any way he could from Amarillo.

Tyler wanted to call Darrel Emerson from her motel room that evening but decided to wait until she had more facts. She did call Brook's father and told him of the group's suspicions giving him her phone number in Las Vegas. "Please keep us informed if the police can find out more about the car or the driver that hit Brook."

While relaxing in the motel's swimming pool that afternoon, Tyler recalled all the information shared by Brook's friends and classmates at breakfast. The students from RIT were upset with the accident and pledged to keep pressing campus officials for more answers.

Sunday would be an all day drive from Dallas to Amarillo leaving early as the sunrise transformed the brown desert sand into a reddish glowing arid region. Texas has many arroyos in its baron landscape causing rough and irregular surfaces that are almost dull but interesting country. The endless flat highway encouraged Tyler's new BMW to speed beyond the limits of normal driving.

Driving 80 mph really did not make much of a difference in the colossal drive. It took five to six hours depending on how many outbreaks of rain she would encounter.

After checking into the Best Western in Amarillo, Tyler called Sam to arrange for the two of them to meet Monday morning at nine AM near the old attorney's office on Ninth Avenue.

The young athlete then changed her clothes and relaxed for about an hour in the indoor swimming pool before retiring for the evening. She remembered the last time she was in that same pool with Darrel Emerson and how their amorous playing continued throughout that night.

Nine months ago, Tyler Castor was a young, naive college graduate believing and trusting Emerson, who was her employer. He was a sexually forceful older man who was married and had acquired a lot of money. It was the same story with all of the men she met while traveling for Redstone Capital, as she presented the investment opportunity at the most expensive country clubs in North America.

Unfortunately, it took a lot of energy to fend off those sexual prowlers who offered her a world of luxury. She had to stay focused in her purpose and knew that she had a good thing with Darrel. However, Tyler's recent discovery of Emerson's possible fraudulent partnership agreements with her and her A&M

colleagues would probably destroy her relationship with the 'nice guy from Minnesota.'

It was hard for Tyler to imagine Emerson causing Brook Madison's death over as simple a transaction as patent rights. In her investigation, she would try to keep an open mind and allow herself to continue trusting in Darrel. However, he was conniving, dishonest and deceptive in his business dealings with investors, business partners and, of course, with his wife of ten years.

In the playground for wealthy men, she was determined not to trust anyone. She listened to her instincts and always would have an exit plan. Emerson would be her first springboard into a wealthy prosperous life without any dependence on a husband or sugar daddy. Becoming self-reliant would be her escape giving her freedom from depending on anyone else.

———————

Tyler was waiting in her luxury sports car as Sam Wade pulled in behind her at curbside. She greeted him as they both headed up the stairs to Andrew Chatsworth's law office on the second floor.

Sam was anxious, nervous and apprehensive letting Tyler take the lead as they proceeded through the office door. Chatsworth was surprised to see the duo but knew who they were. He especially remembered the strikingly attractive blonde graduate student as he smiled from under his big Texas mustache.

"Well, well... I've been expecting one of you A&M grads to visit me. What took you so long?" the lawyer questioned them as he waved them to sit at his big oak round table near the old roll-top desk.

Tyler responded, "If you were expecting us, then why do you question our presence? Maybe we should ask you if you have any fiduciary responsibilities to us. We are here to review the original partnership agreements that Darrel Emerson and you drafted for all of us to sign. We also want copies of the patent registrations that you filed on behalf of us all. We want any corporate filings, land leases and rental agreements you may have written for the Red Rover Project. We also want to see the Red Rover, the gold extracting machine we invented at A&M."

It was not often that the old lawyer found himself intimidated by any woman but the Oklahoma gal was quite assertive, uncommon in Western Texas. She was serious.

The old attorney replied with a condescending voice, "I have bad news for you. I do not have any documents here. If you had called before coming to Amarillo and barging into my office, I would have told you that Mr. Emerson requested all documents be sent to his office in Minnesota for tax reasons. I did exactly that in January. I can call old man Haugan for you and have him meet you at his storage garage where the machine is stored. If you want me to join you, I'll have to charge you my going hourly rate of $150. Once Mr. Emerson paid his bill and requested all legal documents shipped to him, I have no legal obligation to any of you. However, if you want, we can draw up papers while you are here."

Tyler responded, "Mr. Chatsworth, we suspect that Mr. Emerson misled us in those partnership agreements and the patent applications that you wrote for him. You witnessed Emerson's review of the documents and both of you encouraged us to sign. If we were to hire an attorney, it certainly would be someone we could trust. You, sir, facilitated Emerson's fraud and his misrepresentation that may cost you your legal practice."

Chatsworth stood up to intimidate the college students and commented, "Ok, this meeting is over. You can find your machine without my help. Good day. Please leave or I'll call the sheriff."

The college graduates excused themselves from the old lawyer's office. As they stopped by their cars to discuss their next move, Tyler noticed Chatsworth was watching them from his office window.

Tyler spoke first, "Sam, didn't you go with Emerson to store the Red Rover before returning the van last August? Can you recall where the storage facility might be located?"

Sam was reluctant to answer her, "Ya, I think I can find the storage building but maybe we should call Haugan before we go over there."

She replied, "Sam, you lead the way and I'll follow you in my car. I want to see the place before we contact Haugan."

Sam got into his older model Nova and headed south to State Highway 40, which used to be Route 66 years ago. At Big

Texan Road, Sam turned north passing by the Big Texan Steak House and soon after turned into a warehouse and parking area that stored old semi-trailers. Around behind the first building, he stopped by a series of one-level brick garages.

As Tyler drove up, she noticed an old model Chevy pickup truck had parked near the fourth garage door where Sam had stopped. It looked like old man Haugan had just arrived as an eddy of dust settled near his vehicle.

When Tyler approached the two men, they quit talking and greeted her.

Haugan spoke up before Tyler could. "Andy Chatsworth called me and alerted me to your inquiry and told me you wanted to get into my garage. Therefore, I assumed you would be here. I have a key to the padlock; there's no need to break in."

Tyler thought to herself, 'Small towns are all the same. Everyone knows when strangers are around. Everyone knows everyone's business.' However, this known fact might help them in the end.

Observing the area, Tyler realized they were near the warehouse that Emerson had leased last summer for their center of operations. Driving past Big Texan Steak House, she recognized the restaurant as Emerson's favorite dining place when eating with the excavation team. The executive from Minnesota liked the place because it was like sitting in an old John Wayne movie set. Old cowboy memorabilia was on all the walls from years past.

Tyler and her colleagues shared many meals at this 1950's landmark after those gruesome, dirty, hot summer days testing the Red Rover for Emerson.

It was near high noon with temperatures in the 90's as Haugan unlocked the heavy chained sliding door for their inquisitive eyes. At first, the darkness of the enclosed garage covered the entire opening as they looked towards the rear wall. Eventually they could see a brown tarp draped over what looked like the Red Rover machine.

Tyler ventured inward to lift the covering and found a dozen cardboard boxes piled on a pallet. The boxes were full of reddish sand that the engineers had excavated from the Red River last year.

She let out a scream of anger, "Darrel Emerson you lying deceiving snake. Where is our invention? Where is the Red Rover? Mr. Haugan how can this be possible? When were you in here last?"

Haugan walked in cautiously and commented, "Listen here. Mr. Emerson paid for renting the garage for one year. I am not responsible for the whereabouts of any contents that may or may not have been stored in here. Renters can move their property in or out at any time. It's none of my business."

The old Texas property owner continued, "Come September 1, anything left in this building will be hauled to the dump. Have a good day and good luck kids."

Sam Wade stood silent while Tyler stomped around in a fit of anger. All he could say was, "Tyler, let's get out of here. The weatherman is predicting a huge dust storm blowing in from the desert later this afternoon. If you have plans for leaving town today, you had better hit the road going north."

Tyler stopped her temper tantrum. "OK, Sam. I do need to get going. If you find out anything, let me know. I will confront Darrel when I see him in Vegas next week. I doubt if anyone from around here saw anything."

As Tyler Castor drove into Las Vegas, she decided not to alert Darrel to her arrival but instead drove directly to her condo. He was not expecting her to be in Nevada for a couple of days, which gave her time to continue her secret investigation relating to Brook's death and the disappearance of the Red Rover.

She knew Emerson would be in their corporate office during working hours so she slipped in later that evening to poke around Emerson's files.

She would see Emerson in the office tomorrow.

"Good morning, Darrel," Tyler Castor greeted her boss as she entered his office unexpectedly.

"Well, good morning Tyler. How was your trip to Dallas?" Emerson responded with a pleasant smile. "When did you get back? I thought you would let me know so we could be together. I've missed you. I've really missed you."

"Darrel, I had some things to take care of in Texas and after the long drive back, I simply crashed at my place. You know how I get when I'm tired. I'm not very social. My trip was informative... the funeral was sad... you should have been there, you know!"

The blonde haired woman then suggested. "Darrel lets have dinner tonight. I have a lot to share with you. Afterwards, you can come over to my place for a swim and stay the night. We do need to catch up. I need to get to work now. I'm sure a lot has happened during my absence. I think I will schedule an office meeting over lunch with catered sandwiches brought in for the staff. Will you attend?"

"Yes, just let me know the time. It'll be good for everyone to connect and get you back in the loop of things around here," the CEO replied.

Emerson continued, "I'm working on a new limited partnership plan to attract new clients. We will be divesting our holdings out of real estate in the next couple of weeks. The government is starting to clamp down on REITs throughout the country and the IRS wants investment bankers to disclose our

Living in a Lie

clients and our tax shelters. I read the other day the Justice Department is getting involved and demanding offshore banks show their books. This is going to change many private investment portfolios. So, pretty woman get caught up... the next few weeks will be intense."

––––––––––––

After a day of activities, meetings and management directives, Tyler was the last to leave Redstone Venture Capital Investment's office by turning off the lights around six o'clock. She was looking forward to dining with her lover and relaxing in her swimming pool.

She knew in her heart she needed to confront her partner about Brook's unexpected death and the missing Red Rover gold extracting machine with caution.

––––––––––––

Darrel rang Tyler's doorbell precisely at seven-thirty as planned. They greeted each other with a huge lingering French kiss. As their passion boiled over, Tyler pushed Darrel away and suggested they leave for dinner immediately.

He conceded as he stood back to admire his beautiful blonde partner and paramour. She was dressed in a backless silver evening gown which shimmered in the foyer lights. He could almost see through the thin silk dress but she had on a mini-slip and a camisole. As Tyler stepped outside, she intimated

Darrel with her three-inch high-heels and her sexy long legs in natural colored nylons. He noticed she was wearing the large pearl necklace he gave her last Christmas, which accentuated her young cleavage.

WOW !

Darrel Emerson was a handsome, clean-shaven executive wearing a camel colored Italian silk sport coat, white on white stripped silk dress shirt, navy blue silk dress pants with brown Italian leather loafers and no socks. He was an athletic man in his early thirties with light brown curly hair. Most people who noticed him assumed he was a model for GQ magazine.

His friends at the local country club describe Emerson as 'a gentleman's gentle man.' Everyone knew him to be well-educated, successful and a wealthy investment banker. People in Las Vegas did not know that he was a married man with two teenage daughters living in Minnesota.

———————

The couple slid into their private booth at Andre's in downtown Vegas, ready to enjoy an expensive dinner with wine.

Tyler began her investigation into Brook Madison's death and the disappearance of the Red Rover. Darrel choked on his first sip of wine as the lovely goddess asked him questions unexpectedly.

"Darrel, do you know why Brook was murdered at RIT a couple of weeks ago in Rochester?"

He responded with shock, "No, why would I? Matter of fact, I really have no idea what has been going on with your college friends. Maybe you should clue me in."

Tyler proceeded to reveal all that had happened with Brook, Sam and Sally and their conversations in Dallas. She closed her dissertation by disclosing her meetings with Chatsworth and old man Haugan in Amarillo.

Emerson seemed shocked and became very defensive denying all suspicions and involvement surrounding Brook's death and the disappearance of Red Rover. "I can't believe it, Tyler, that you would think I could cause someone's death and then steal Red Rover from my partners."

"I do not know anything about these crimes. I was in Minnesota with my wife and daughters when Brook was killed. Yes, I did request all the legal documents be sent to my Minnesota office for safekeeping and for tax records. You certainly can have copies of our agreements and as far as the patent registrations, our partnership agreement secures yours and the others ownership. In addition, why in the world would I want the Red Rover when you and I are making millions of dollars with Redstone Investments?"

Emerson continues his defense, "Someone else is behind this... no doubt a desperate person that needs the money. I would be shocked to find out if the Red Rover was worth anything. Granted, I made over a million dollars in fees with the investment portfolio. Why would I take that gold extracting machine especially, when the price of gold is still below market?"

Tyler backed off her interrogation and thought about Darrel's comments. "You can certainly understand why we have our suspicions."

Darrel suggested. "I'll tell you what I'll do. I know a guy in Minnesota who can investigate the disappearance of the Red Rover and possibly, Brook's death. If both incidences are connected, I'll let you know when he reports back to me. Let's relax and enjoy the evening. We can't solve these mysteries tonight."

She replied with acceptance, "You are right... nothing can be done tonight. However, please keep me informed. I will not tell Sam and Sally about your investigator yet. I'll just tell them we were wrong about you and they will be getting copies of all the partnership agreements that we all signed."

Tyler and Darrel agreed not to discus anymore business that evening and began their romantic ritual of seducing each other. They were both hungry for passion.

Emerson woke to the ringing of his telephone at two o'clock in the early morning on July 1. I called him to confirm our scheduled meeting at the Cosmopolitan Hotel on July 3, 1981.

I whispered, "I'll be staying at the Cosmo. Call my room when you arrive in the lobby and then come on up. We'll have more privacy there. I'll expect you around five o'clock. Okay?"

Living in a Lie

Emerson replied, "That works for me. I'll expect good news. See ya then."

Two days later Darrel Emerson filled a briefcase with $100,000 in cash and set the combination locks before leaving his safe-deposit box. This would be his first transfer of assets with me if everything went as planned. Emerson would be stashing ten times that amount over the next six months if he could trust me.

Emerson called my room from the lobby phone and continued his mission to the tenth floor, room 1019, where I was waiting with the door open.

"Any problems?" I asked.

"No problems and no one knows of my activities. I've got a hundred grand in this briefcase and my next transfer will be a million if everything goes as planned. Do you have the account numbers? Did you follow my instructions?" Emerson spoke carefully.

"Ya, I've opened nine separate accounts in nine different banks on the Cayman Islands. Each of the banks charged a $500 fee for opening each account. Here is the information and account numbers. You'll be able to transfer money in and out through wire transfers. However, be careful. Do not leave a paper trail. I'll meet you on September 3 in Minneapolis. I'll be staying at the Curtis Hotel with all your deposit receipts, an itemization of my costs and plans to travel to the Cayman Islands again. So far, you owe me $25,000 for my services and $7,500 for expenses. Do you have that with you?"

"Ya, I have it in this airline's travel bag," Emerson replied but was quick to ask his confidant. "What about the other problem I need resolved?"

I responded, "I haven't taken any action yet to protect you from being a suspect. I need to plan this carefully. Do you have any ideas? Will she be traveling out of the country someday soon?"

Emerson had a suggestion, "Her birthday is coming up in August. I'll buy tickets for her and her sister to take a cruise in the Caribbean in September. Will that help?"

"Good idea. Let me know the details and then I'll take action," I replied.

"Hey Red, I want you to look into the disappearance of a gold extracting machine that I had stored in Amarillo for the past year. Someone removed it without my knowledge and without any trace," Emerson explained.

The two of men exchanged the details, which would help begin the investigation and my next assignment. Emerson left the hotel room undetected after meeting for an hour. The less time we spend together, the better.

For the next two months, Emerson, Tyler and their highly trained staff initiated Redstone's next investment portfolio.

First, all the investors in the Red Earth Properties, LLC would be notified that the REIT was closing due to new changes in government regulations and by the SEC. The tax shelters Red Earth offered Investors were under investigation by the IRS. Rather than taking a chance of exposing their wealthy shareholders to unneeded scrutiny, Redstone encouraged their investors to rollover (reinvest) their money into a new startup business venture called Redwood Industries, LLC.

Red Earth Properties would close all accounts and records while their investors' money was transferred to a Las Vegas bank; held in escrow until distribution could be re-established through a private channel. On the other hand, Redstone could rollover their investor's money immediately into Redwood Industries.

Redwood was a new startup business incorporated in West Palm Beach, Florida with the purpose of developing a new product for building all weather decks and fences. It was a patented process of recycling cardboard, old rubber tires and discarded cooking grease from fast food restaurants. The recycled materials were ground into small particles; mixed with sticky grease; heated to a boil; poured into cooling molds with a textured wood finish 3-inches wide by 96-inches long and then sold to consumers through major building product retailers.

The inventor was a recent graduate engineering student from the University of Florida who invented the all weather product for his thesis. Redwood Industries held nine patents, which Redstone Venture Capital purchased, and needed millions of investment dollars in order to begin manufacturing and distribution of the artificial wood boards.

Tyler Castor flew to Florida to take photographs of the manufacturing process and to interview the inventor. The staff in Vegas created a beautiful portfolio for mailing to the private group of investors. As soon as Tyler's photos were processed and inserted, the marketing materials were printed and sent to the wealthy clients.

A minimum investment of $10,000,000 was required. Redstone would charge a minimum filing fee of two percent with a five percent commission on capital gains when the preferred stock sold.

The purchase of the initial offering of ownership shares would be available until October 1, 1981. After that date, only common stock would be available. Redstone Venture anticipated filing an initial public stock offering (IPO) in 1985.

Early investors could realize 25% to 30% return when selling their preferred stock. Common stock might render a 15% to 20% gain.

––––––––––

After flying to the Cayman Islands, depositing Emerson's money ($10,000 evenly into the nine secret bank accounts), I changed my itinerary. Instead of returning to Minnesota, I purchased a one-way ticket in Miami and then flew to Dallas.

Living in a Lie

I rented a car and headed north on I-35 to Oklahoma City. Two hours later I headed west on I-40 to Amarillo where I checked into the Best Western near the airport. I was tired of driving all day, seeing nothing but red desert sand.

It was early morning, around seven, when I woke to see the sun rising over the historic city anticipating another hot, dry summer day. After eating breakfast in the lobby restaurant, I checked out, packed the car, drove five miles south to the town of Canyon and parked in front of the A&M University Administrative Building.

I went directly to the office for Student Records asking the clerk if I could review the personnel files of the four graduate engineers that worked on the Gold Extracting Machine in 1980. I convinced her to give up the information by stating, "I'm here from Gas, Oil and Minerals National Magazine. I'm hoping to interview one or all of the inventors for a relevant article I'm writing."

"I'm hoping to contact them at their last known address in order to interview them before writing the article," I forged my phony story to appease the academic sentinel.

The clerk wrote down the last known address for all four students and included their parents' addresses and the student's home high school just in case I needed more info. It was easier than I expected. I guess by being respectful and kind to people they will be more generous in their efforts to help.

I discover from the list that Sam Wade recently moved to Houston after finishing his Masters in Engineering at A&M. His hometown address was not in the admissions records nor did he have any relatives living in Texas. It seemed odd but sometimes details are secret for personal reasons.

Before leaving Amarillo, I called old man Haugan to ask him some key questions about the storage garage where Red Rover was kept. His answers were not helpful.

I drove back to Dallas that afternoon under cloudy skies and temperatures in the 80's. Texas is boring along the Interstate highways.

I had more to do before returning to Minnesota so I stayed the night at the Warwick Melrose Hotel in Dallas. The next morning I would drive to Houston and search for the two A&M students, Sam Wade and Sally Livingston.

My hunt for Red Rover was not over.

Tyler Castor was very efficient and precise at her job of Vice President, checking every detail of Redstone's staff as the Redwood Investment Portfolio was completed. Her major pet peeve was typos and punctuation in the business copy of the marketing materials.

Her photographs were stunning examples for using natural lighting to create drama and high contrast for holding the viewer's attention. The investors who viewed these high quality brochures were impressed with the imagery that emphasized the redwood looking decks, highlighting the modern manufacturing equipment while showing the molding process of liquefied rubber compound.

This graduated engineer, skilled photographer and competent business editor made the marketing department excel beyond all expectations. Ms. Castor would have been successful with her own advertising and marketing firm in New York City if she had wanted.

Emerson knew Tyler was crucial to Redstone's success. On the other hand, he could replace her for half the money she was getting in salary and benefits. If it were not for the amorous benefits he enjoyed with this twenty-five year old college graduate, he could save a quarter of million dollars annually.

When the Redstone's promotional packages were mailed out, the investment dollars came in by the millions. The quality presentation conveyed confidence, reliance and trust. Redstone's reputation assured the venture to be unfailing with enormous returns.

The duo did it again. Emerson's creative ideas and Castor's creative talents made them a lot of money. All of the investors in the Red Earth LLC did roll their dollars into Redwood Industries without any hesitation. With a 'blink of an eye,' one hundred million dollars was in Redstone's bank account in Nevada and eventually transferred into a bank in Miami.

Now was the best time for Emerson to execute his secret surreptitious strategy to protect his assets and begin investing in his own personal retirement.

My next meeting with Emerson would elevate him into the lofty category of one of the largest tax dodgers in US history. What he was about to do was against the law and immoral. Nevertheless, as his confidant and offshore executor, it was my responsibility to do what he wanted and keep my mouth shut.

I am only the carrier pigeon not the eagle.

We met as planned in Minneapolis, at the Curtis Hotel, in a private suite on September 3. Emerson seemed a little nervous and uneasy so I inquired, "How are things going in Vegas?"

The executive responded, "My worries are not in Vegas for now. In this suitcase is the first of five deposits that you are to deposit evenly in those nine bank accounts in the Cayman Islands. There is ten million bucks in here. Herring, I'm trusting you to get this done without any questions or problems. After you complete this assignment, fly to Miami and board this cruise liner." He hands me a travel brochure and continues, "You will have seven days of basking in the sun while traveling to and from Barbados. When the ship begins its return trip to the US, you are to dispose of my problem into the Caribbean Sea. I do not need to tell you what to do afterwards."

I replied with a complete understanding of what he wanted. "I will not have any communications with you, whatsoever, until January 5th, when I will meet you in Atlanta. I'll be prepared to make another trip to the Cayman Islands the week afterwards. My fees have now added up to $50,000, at that time."

I then disclosed the information I had on the disappearance of the Red Rover invention. "Here's what I found out about that gold extracting machine. In March of this year, the machine was removed from the storage garage in Amarillo, transported by van to an obscure ranch outside of Houston and then it was sold to a group of businessmen from Guatemala who own large deposits of gold."

I continue to share my findings with Emerson. "It seems a graduate engineer, Sam Wade, a student from A&M, used one of your investment brochures to sell the Red Rover through a machinery broker in Tijuana, Mexico. The broker's name was Miguel Carlos, aka, Mickey Carter who sold the Red Rover for $100,000, keeping $10,000 as sales commission. Carter then charged the businessmen another $10,000 as a finder's fee. The machine was crated up in Houston, shipped to Belize, then trucked overland to the ore mines in Guatemala. The price of gold is now 200% higher than it is in the US."

"My contacts in Mexico tell me that this Carter guy has moved to Minnesota and purchased rental properties in North Minneapolis," I rendered my report.

"Sam Wade moved to Houston and lives at the same address as another A&M grad by the name of Sally Livingston. I tracked her down to interview her. She was surprised that I found her and was reluctant to answer my questions. When I asked about Wade, she told me he was in Central America on a six-month consultant job as an engineer. And then she closed the door in my face."

"I decided not to get too pushy and scare her into running. I did not ask about her classmate, Brook Madison," I reported.

"Now I can track down this Carter guy in Minnesota if you want. I'll have time in November," I concluded.

Emerson responded, "Let's leave Carter alone until the spring, I have plenty to think about right now. Besides, the Red Rover is gone and I do not have a claim on Carter's cut but I might confront the A&M students after Wade comes back to the US."

"Ok, thanks. Do you have any questions about your next assignment?" Emerson concluded the meeting.

We parted as Darrel Emerson left the hotel suite and took the elevator to the parking garage in the basement level.

No one knew of our meeting.

"Hello, I'm calling for Colleen Williams," Tyler inquired.

The voice on the telephone responded, "Yes it is. Who's calling?"

"This is Tyler Castor, remember me? We met at Brook Madison's funeral in Dallas last year."

"Yes, I remember you. I'm glad you called," Colleen responded. "Just this past week, I was cleaning my dorm room and packing to leave RIT for summer break when I came across a sealed envelope with your name on it. I figured it was something that

Brook wanted you to have. If you give me your mailing address I'll mail it you today."

Tyler quickly responded, "By all means. I will look for it in a couple of days. Did the police find out who hit and killed Brook?"

Colleen was Brook's roommate when the accident happened. She informed Tyler, "No, not a thing has been discovered. The campus police told me a few months ago that the Rochester Police have no leads. It is an unsolved mystery."

After getting Colleen's summer phone number, Tyler said goodbye and hung up wondering what could be in the envelope.

The brown manila envelope arrived on Friday at Tyler's condo in Vegas while she was swimming in her pool. She was anxious to see the contents as she slit open the end. Inside she found another white envelope addressed to her.

After carefully opening the year old envelope, she found a handwritten letter addressed to her by her college friend. It said.

"Tyler, if you are reading this, then something has happened to me. I have a confession to make to you and my family. My father already knows but has not told anyone."

"The last year of college at A&M I got sexually involved with Sally. If you remember, she was my roommate that year. Our relationship continued

secretly through the summer while we were all working for Darrel Emerson in Amarillo. Every Saturday, when you and Sam worked at the warehouse cleaning the truck and Red Rover, Sally, and I were supposed to be cleaning the house, we would enjoy our time together in bed. We were very cautious not to let anyone know, especially Sam. He had expectations to marry Sally after he finished his Masters. Sally was afraid Sam would freak out and break off their relationship. So we kept it a secret."

The ambiguous letter continued...

"Tyler, when I started at RIT in September, after we finished the Red Rover project, my roommate Colleen and I became lovers. I felt I had to tell Sally. I called her and informed her that I would not be involved with her over my winter break. She was distraught by the news and demanded that I say nothing to Sam about our affair."

Tyler continued reading Brook's admissions.

"I also felt it was important for me to tell my parents over the Christmas Holiday when I returned to Dallas. My mother was shocked and cried for

days. My father was silent. I know he is concerned that if my revelation comes out in the news, his political career will be over. My father is a very conservative Christian who consistently speaks out against the GLBT lifestyle. He was very angry at me for being so selfish."

"So, now you know what has happened in my life. I know Sally is very angry and bitter towards me. I do not think she will hurt me because she really loves me. However, my father is righteous in his self-serving resentment. He has disowned me and will not support me anymore."

"If something terrible has happened to me, I would expect my father hired someone to silence me. Please do not divulge this information as it will hurt both Sally and Colleen."

The last line closed the letter forever.

"God will judge my father for what he has done. Brook Madison. April, 1982."

Chapter Five

Cunning Confessions

May, 1986...

"FATHER, FORGIVE ME FOR I have sinned", Darrel Emerson bowed his head in reverence as he knelt before the altar in the Waterville Catholic Church.

It had been a long time since the 40 year old man felt any contrition for his sins and to abjure for his deceitful ways. He had come home to the church that baptized him. The same church he was first married and where his two daughters were baptized. It was in the same small town church his parents were married in along with his two uncles and three of his four brothers.

Darrel's relatives were known throughout the community and within the Catholic Church. The other parishioners in the congregation knew which pews the Emerson family occupied

Living in a Lie

every Sunday morning, Easter morning, Christmas Eve and on Christmas morning.

When the church membership needed to raise money for special projects, the entire Emerson clan donated more money than any other group or family. It was a rumor that Darrel's father, George Emerson, the family patriarch, gave a new black Buick to the monsignor every two years.

Every year during Lent, the Emerson family delivered a truck load of fresh food to the ladies of the church, the Altar and Rosary Society, for feeding the poor in the area.

The church men's group, The Holy Name Society, would distribute new bibles to local motels and hotels that were within a fifty mile radius, funded solely by George Emerson, every year.

If a poor family in town needed to bury a relative and did not have the funds, Darrel's uncle William would provide his services as a mortician without charge. The other uncle, Harvey, who owned the only bank in town, would purchase a grave site and pay for an etched tombstone.

The family farm where Darrel grew up had a large grove of evergreen trees that provided freshly cut blue spruce trees during Christmas; for the church, the parsonage, the bank, the funeral home and the senior citizen's home.

Every Thanksgiving the entire clan would get together at the family homestead to give thanks and report to George how much they gave to charity and to the schools throughout the past year.

All of Darrel's relatives, their children and grandchildren knew grandpa Emerson's homily, "Those that are blessed with the rewards of life must give to those that are without. The Bible says, Give unto others and you will receive more blessings from God."

Darrel's success as a businessman afforded him the highest ranking in the family and he was the greatest benefactor to the local church and the New Ulm Diocese. Every year he donated thousands of dollars to the Sodality Fund to help with the youth programs in the church. Money was donated to the local chapter of the Knights of Columbus and special contributions were given to the Archdiocese Appeal Fund, the Building Fund and the Cemetery Fund.

Darrel purchased many of the newest pews in the sanctuary on behalf of Emerson relatives, noted with gold engraved plaques fastened to both ends of the solid oak benches.

On Mother's Day, the church sanctuary glistened with hundreds of white lilies provided by Darrel and his four brothers commemorating their grandmother and their mother.

There was no doubt that Darrel James Emerson was the wealthiest person to live in Waterville, Minnesota. His name appeared on bronze plaques in the elementary school, the high school and in the local hospital.

No one in the Emerson family, the church or in the community, would have expected Darrel to be making amends for any misdeeds or disgraceful behavior. Everyone admired him.

Father Michael Benson stood in the sanctuary watching the church's benefactor crying while kneeling at the communion rail. The priest immediately recognized the man knowing the parishioner had not been worshipping in the church for the past five years.

"My son, you are always welcome. Do you wish to have Confession or would you like to meet with me in my chambers?" Father Benson broke the silence in the sanctuary.

"Father Benson, I think it would be best if we meet in private. Do you have time for me now?" Darrel questioned the man of God.

The patriarch of the small town church held out his hand directing the troubled man to a private office through a door on the left. Emerson followed the priest into the inner sanctum of the religious buildings, remembering the days when he was an acolyte as a teenager permitted into the secretive rooms behind the altar.

Only a few parishioners were invited into Father Benson's personal office for private consultations. It was an honor, almost sanctimonious.

"Mr. Emerson, what is troubling you? How can I ease your pain, my son?" the Holy Father began their session of absolution.

"Father, my life is not what it seems. My parents and my family have no idea how tenuous my businesses have been. Those who have trusted me and believed in my investments have been misled and betrayed hoping to increase their prosperity," the esteemed businessman began his confession.

"For over the last five years, I swindled millions of dollars from wealthy investors who will not realize any financial gain nor will they get their initial principle returned. I have created the illusions of prosperity by hiding my loses, transferring my assets and avoiding any accountability," the broken man repented his deceptive practices.

"In my pursuit to become a wealthy, respected and an admired businessman, I have lied to those I love, I have betrayed my daughters and deceived the church. God have mercy on my soul. I have broken every commandment from God. My soul is doomed to hell," the cunning mortal confessed his sins.

The priest folded his hands, bowed his head, "My son, let us pray and ask God to forgive you and ease your sorrow.

———————

Father Benson spent more then an hour with Darrel listening to him witness his unsavory life. A life of lies, conning money out of those who trusted his investment advice, unknowingly being suckered into a never ending cycle of broken promises.

The conniving criminal finally admitted his deceptive life asking God for mercy upon his soul. Father Benson then encouraged Emerson to change his life of crime by asking his family for forgiveness and to return the money taken from investors.

"You must make amends before God sincerely," the priest explained. "When you begin to admit your sins your life will change. You must kneel and humble yourself before those you love and ask for their forgiveness."

   "God will forgive you if you are honest and true to your words," the priest spoke with conviction. "You can change your life from this day forth."

Darrel Emerson wept in sorrow as the priest spoke softly encouraging him to pay penance and atone for his sins. "Begin your recovery by giving all of your earthly possessions to God."

"Praise to the Lord for he is my salvation," the sinner prayed silently.

At that moment, Darrel Emerson asked Father Benson, "How can I help the church and praise God?"

"My son, you must begin renewing your life by donating to the church. Your life will have purpose with your abundant generosity for paying homage to the Archdiocese's Appeal Fund today?"

———————

Darrel James Emerson repented and escaped from Purgatory for a measly payment of one million dollars.

Amen.

Chapter Six

Synchronizing Life

September 1991...

DARREL EMERSON AGREED TO MEET his lifelong friend Sara Blake at a restaurant in the Radisson Hotel, near Sara's home in Edenborough, Minnesota.

Sara was lonely again and needed Darrel to comfort her as she begged him to meet. He had many misgivings in seeing her because his second marriage was currently unstable and volatile for many reasons.

It was eleven o'clock on Friday morning, when the couple met for lunch. They embraced and kissed in their private booth near the rear of the secluded restaurant. The last time they had been together was in December 1989 when Darrel took Sara and her kids to a local indoor mall. Back then, Sara needed to talk with her high school boy friend and first lover about her pending divorce from Morgan Blake.

Two years had passed so she needed to bring Emerson up-to-date about her escape from her marriage by reviewing all the bitter details of the many court battles and how her estranged husband, Morgan Blake, had been arrested three times while stalking her. Hennepin County finally convicted him of terrorist threats, attempted homicide and then sentenced him to 18 months in prison. In addition, a US Federal Court had recently dismissed charges against Morgan for conspiracy of arson and for insurance fraud after the government's star witness disappeared.

She told her confidant, "Morgan Blake's release would be on October 1 from the Hennepin County Correctional Facility. He will be very angry and will take revenge against her. Sara knew her pious ex-husband hated her for the rebellion and for their legal battles, including her claims to his deceased twin brother's estate."

Emerson listened patiently; Sara would be facing many unresolved issues including visitation, garnishment of child support, division of marital property and hopefully, her share of the fire insurance payout. It would be years before all their battles would be resolved, as neither litigant would concede to the other.

Her children were angry with their parents for not reconciling their differences. It was hard for Sara to imagine how her five children would survive their unsettled and hateful memories of their fanatical father and their terrible life on the farm in Freedom, Illinois.

The meeting between Sara Harrison-Blake and Darrel Emerson was bitter sweet as they commiserated with each other over the past twenty-five years of disappointment, loneliness and broken dreams.

Darrel began to reconstruct his past by sharing the events of building his investment business and becoming a wealthy millionaire. He expressed remorse over losing his first wife in her accidental death while she was on a cruise with her sister in 1981.

He continued telling Sara how his prosperity changed after his wife's death. His two daughters became distraught, angry and defiant as he traveled to and from Las Vegas to manage his investment firm. Eventually, he purchased a luxury home in West Palm Beach and hid away while trying to resurrect his failing business, Redwood Industries.

Emerson agonized over his mounting losses and huge debts, while his ex-partner, Tyler Castor, began a new life of luxury after resigning from Redstone in the mid 1980's. She met an auto mogul in Las Vegas while he was visiting from Minnesota. After dating long distance for about six months, she moved to Minnesota to marry him and become involved in his business.

Tyler had convinced Emerson to buy her stock in their Redhead Partnership in order to keep her from disclosing his secret cache in the Cayman Islands. He paid her a million bucks to sell out and leave Redstone Investments. Darrel later learned that Tyler invested her money in a startup business called Redstar Enterprises, which leased new automobiles to a national rental car agency that had

Living in a Lie

locations at every major airport in the US. The enterprise was the first auto rental center in the country to be located at major US airports. Redstar dominated the industry for years.

Sara listened as her high school boy friend from Waterville, Minnesota told her of his problems with the IRS for unpaid taxes and with the SEC for investment fraud. His stockholders were hunting for him. He anticipated a rancher from Montana might have hired a hit man to kill him.

Emerson's tax free investment schemes were all 'red herring' investments and illegal. However, as the US Justice Department rifled through his firm's records in Minnesota, they were demanding to search through all the records at Redstone Investments in Las Vegas. That is when his empire began falling apart.

The executive's only assets were his condominiums in Mexico and Nevada, his personal homes in Florida and Minnesota. However, he recently transferred the properties to his two daughters and his second wife in 1989.

The one time multi-millionaire was living on thin air without any financial parachutes to save him from total ruin. He did not disclose nor would he consider withdrawing any of his secret untaxed cache stashed in offshore bank accounts. He never told anyone about the millions stowed away in the Cayman Islands and he was not about to tell his hometown girl friend, Sara.

He recounted how his great prosperity began with his brilliant scheme called Red Rover. It was the first of many unsecured frauds that made him a wealthy man. He told her how the gold extracting invention disappeared from a storage garage in Amarillo in 1981 and then it sold and shipped it to an unknown location in Central America. The graduated student from A&M, Sam Wade, sold the Red Rover through a machinery broker and had it shipped to the ore mines in Guatemala. Wade was hired to train the miners in operating the one of a kind machine.

A private investigator hired by Emerson later discovered that the Central American Government eventually executed Wade for fraud and deception. The machine never worked. The initial outlay of $100,000 for the 'Rube Goldberg' was gone and never recovered.

All that had happened over the last five years left him without any backup resources forcing him into bankruptcy. He was penniless and needed to start over... that was the story he told Sara.

As their midday luncheon became an all day affair, the couple rented a room for the night. They both wanted to rekindle their sexual desires and were ready and eager to resume their lost relationship from twenty-five years ago. As they commiserated over a second bottle of wine, Darrel proclaimed his marriage was over and Sara wanted him to be her paramour once again.

That night Darrel Emerson gave up his marriage and committed himself to Sara Harrison-Blake. They spent the night pleasing each other with amorous affection and vowed to be together as soon as Darrel could divorce his second wife, Amy.

Without Darrel ever knowing, Sara called his wife the next afternoon insisting she divorce her husband. After all, Sara was his first lover and the Emerson's marriage was 'on the rocks.' When Amy Emerson answered the phone that fateful day, the voice on the other end divulged confidential and intimate details about the rendezvous her husband had the night before. Sara did everything she could to convince the married woman that it was 'God's plan' for Darrel to leave his marriage and be with Sara. Within 24 hours, Mrs. Emerson filed for divorce and forced her husband to leave their home.

Sara was ready and willing to help Darrel, encouraging him to move into her four-bedroom home so they could start a new life together.

Darrel Emerson took advantage of Sara's offer and then convinced her to leverage the equity in her home and invest it in a joint LLC. She would be the registered CEO in all government documentation. She was able to obtain a second mortgage of $80,000 on her home and deposited it into a private bank account in Nevada.

If Emerson could 'lay low' for a couple of months until his divorce was final, he would be able to start up a new venture preventing his creditors from finding him during the interim. He had been working on an innovative idea and knew that Sara Blake could help market the venture by selling preferred stock to major investors before offering the public stock through an IPO.

Darrel told Sara, "Sara, this is how I became a multi-millionaire in 1980 and we can do it again together. I can leverage $50,000 in a startup venture in South Dakota by selling the investment opportunity to wealthy cattle ranchers and within six months we'll be rich."

Emerson's intuitive instincts for selecting a naive colleague, proved to be shrewd and prudent. Tyler Castor had coerced many wealthy investors with her charm, her angelic appearance and her perceptive business wisdom. Tyler came from money and the 'Country Club Crowd'; she could talk their talk and walk their walk to gain their trust.

Sara had all those same attributes in addition to her Christian values that made her more believable and compelling. This innocent pretty woman, mother of five kids, grew up in a small town in Minnesota; had raised cattle and dogs on a farm in Illinois and knew the Bible better than any Christian conservative farmer in the upper Midwest.

She was sincere, genuine in her communication skills and somewhat flirtatious with men.

He knew Sara would be right for the venture. If she had the chance, she could convince God to buy a signed first edition of the Old Testament for his own personal library.

Living in a Lie

As the two entrepreneurs kick off their new venture capital business, Darrel made a few suggestions to Sara, "In order to give your full attention to our business, maybe you should sell or close your executive recruiting firm. The Internet is starting to connect candidates seeking new employment with companies that have openings through Monster.com and Craig's Lists. It will not be long before your clients create their own employment Web sites bypassing your services altogether to begin competing with you. The investment banking business offers us unlimited opportunities. If we have a sound investment portfolio with an ROI (return on investment) that proves to be profitable, investors will be standing in line to give us lots of money."

"Sara, with your background in sales and marketing, you can learn how to create effective Web sites for presenting our investment firm's portfolio. This new technology will save us money by not printing expensive four-color portfolios," Emerson continues to express his views to Sara.

After listening to Darrel's insightful reasoning, she acquiesces, "Darrel, you are correct. We need to offer unique opportunities on a limited basis to a select few who can afford to invest. Whereas, the Internet now offers many qualified candidates unlimited opportunities, overwhelming human resources with unlimited resumes without much effort. Companies no longer need my intuitive qualities and exclusive candidates will no longer value my confidentiality."

She was ready to take the risk and begin a new career learning the ropes from her new mentor. The Christian woman had always wanted great wealth. The sooner the better. She had lived in near poverty most of her life and it was unlikely she would receive any money from her divorce settlement. Her ex-husband was not paying child support nor would he give up the fight to keep his family's wealth.

"I'm ready and capable to rise above my circumstances and meet all the challenges in order to experience success." The forty-year-old, divorced mother of five children, impoverished by her legal bills, willingly surrendered her worries to her trusted lover.

It was not long before Emerson had his business plan ready to submit to his partner. Even before Redstone went out of business and Redwood Industries stock liquidated, Darrel had already concocted his next money making scheme.

Emerson explained his plans, "Sara, our new investment opportunity will be called Methane Red Gas & Energy, LLC. A graduate student at the University of North Dakota has written his hypothesis on Organic/inorganic Chemistry Theories. He has applied his knowledge in physical chemistry to solve energy problems throughout the world. His recent experiments concluded that methane gas from cattle and hog manure can be converted into energy for fueling heat generated turbines that will produce electricity on remote ranches."

Sara agreed, "I know from my own experience of raising cattle in Illinois, and knowing a little about my ex-husband's family hog

Living in a Lie

business in Iowa, methane gas is very volatile and farmers need to vent their barns with large exhaust fans. I also agree that large ranches need to be self-sufficient and produce their own electricity. Most of these feedlots are located far away from cities and town where it is expensive to have electrical power lines put up."

Darrel then concluded, "Ok, let's setup our business venture in Sioux Falls, South Dakota to raise capital for building gas converters that can be sold to cattle ranchers throughout the Upper Midwest."

Sara added her thoughts, "Darrel, why limit our venture to the Upper Midwest? Let's go global. If we envision manufacturing plants being built in Europe and Asia, wouldn't our venture have greater appeal to larger investors?"

Darrel replied to his protégé, "Sara, you are correct. We'll need huge amounts of startup capital and then we can sell large packages of preferred stock to institutions and investment brokerage firms on Wall Street before creating an IPO. Our fees alone could be over $10,000,000."

Emerson was getting excited listening to their hypothesis and commanded immediate action. "Sara, lets get in contact with Professor Daniel Alberding at UND and fly up to Fargo. Have him meet us at a local motel restaurant. We'll offer to purchase his patents and copyrights and pay him royalties to use his name and processes."

Over the next six months, Sara and Darrel established their new corporate offices, their personal and business bank accounts and a team of special lawyers and they contracted with an ISP in Sioux Falls. Their new business Methane Red Gas & Energy, LLC, was registered with the Secretary of State of South Dakota. Sara wrote Professor Alberding's profile and bio for their new Web site www.goREDindustries.com.

Darrel began writing the prospectus and each page for the Web site while selecting photos to compliment the details. After meeting with their attorney, he had registered trademarks, copyrights and Limited Liability Corporation documents to be on file in their corporate office located in downtown Sioux Falls, on Sixth Street, overlooking the Big Sioux River.

Without Sara knowing, Darrel retained another law firm in Las Vegas to establish a private holding company totally owned by his daughter, Susan Emerson. The Parent Holding Company, Red Energy Development Industries (REDi), would own all the preferred stock in Methane Red Gas & Energy, LLC. Sara had assumed whatever Darrel established was best for the two of them. He was the expert in their business matters.

They were then married in Hawaii in July; she understood that she would be entitled to at least fifty percent, if they would ever divorce.

Living in a Lie

Darrel Emerson was a 'big spender' demanding the best money could buy; a new Lincoln Continental, expensive clothes, always the best restaurants, the best office location in Sioux Falls with expensive contemporary furniture, first class seating in airplanes and the most expensive hotel for their honeymoon. In reality, the money he was spending was Sara's home equity loan. The couple had spent over fifty thousand dollars within their first year together soon to be living on Sara's credit cards. All this time, Sara was supporting her family, paying their monthly expenses, making house payments, paying her divorce attorney for legal bills, trying to payoff her second mortgage while shelling out money for the startup business in South Dakota.

All the time Darrel speculated how much money would be coming into their joint business soon after they began promoting his big plans for Methane Red Gas & Energy.

———————

In September 1992, their Web site was ready to launch and the news would spread quickly through the investment industry. The front page detailed their objectives.

"Methane Red Gas & Energy was creating a private equity fund for Venture Capital Partnerships

to further develop technology relating to oil & gas, power, water, clean energy, as well as biotechnology and new methane gas technology."

"Our Mission is to develop an appropriate venture capital industry infrastructure and community throughout the World, nurturing investment ties between North America, Asia, the European Union as well as Russian Countries."

"Methane Red Gas & Energy will be a Capital Investment Advisory and Venture Capital Management firm specializing in developing new capital markets. MRGE is a South Dakota LLC based in Sioux Falls, representing a group of investors and private developers with a high net worth."

"By focusing on inventions, patents and technical developments, outstanding opportunities can achieve great success," their Web site noted.

"As knowledgeable venture capitalists, we are rational strategists who focus on identifying sectors of the economy where the rate of business change will be the greatest and investment opportunities are most profound."

"The founders of MRGE, Sara Blake-Emerson along with Professor Daniel Alberding, PHD, are working in partnership to join efforts in developing methane gas technologies as clean energy for the future, worldwide."

———————

Sara voiced her concerns to Darrel, "If this business enterprise does not receive investment funds soon, we will not be in business, not even to pay the ISP bill for hosting our Web site. I'm broke, my credit cards are tapped out and our expenses are beyond my resources."

Emerson reassured her by giving her some guidance, "Sara, write up a Press Release and distribute it on the Web and to other Venture Capitalists in my database. We may have to call some of the wealthiest cattle ranchers in the state. Contact the Department of Revenue and get a listing of the largest feedlots and let's do a mailing announcing Professors Alberding's research and our investment opportunity."

He continued his directives, "Sara, do you have any relatives that could invest in our startup business? You could offer them a preferred stockholder position. Do you have any wealthy contacts in the printing industry from your recruiting days that could possibly trade services for preferred stock? It looks like this Internet stuff and Web sites will not work. We'll need to print some portfolios quickly. Do you have any other ideas?"

"Darrel, I have a cousin in the western suburbs of the Twin Cities that has a very successful insurance business who could afford to invest. In addition, I do have personal contacts in the printing industry that might be interested in exchanging printing services for preferred stock," Sara replied with some apprehension.

"Darrel, you are asking me to put my integrity on the line. Can I trust that my family and friends will get their money back and receive some return on the investment?"

"Of course, you can trust me. I have done this before with great success. The first investors get the best position and I promise you they will make money on this deal. Sara, they will be investing in you. In your business. In your future," The conniving man promised his wife.

"Do you have any other ideas?" he asked her.

"Matter of fact, Darrel, I do," she replied. "You assumed that cattle ranchers and hog feedlot owners know about the Internet and would be using the Web. They are _not_ involved in this technology for now. Maybe in ten years they might be. Secondly, in order to gain their trust, you must be part of their community. Most of these successful ranchers and farmers in the Upper Midwest are Christians who go to church on Sundays. These community leaders do _not_ belong to country clubs like in the big cities. Most of them do not have time for golf."

Living in a Lie

"We can gain their trust by meeting them in the pews of their churches. I know these people and they will trust in me. However, the question I have, can you express your Christian faith and convince them that you are a believer so they can trust in you?"

Emerson responded. "Yes, of course I can. I have been a member of the Catholic Church all my life. I know a lot about God and the Bible. In addition, you can be a character reference. You have known me all of your life. You can verify my credentials and my expertise."

Sara advised her second husband cautiously. "My dear husband, if you were to confess your sins and give your life to God and be 'born again,' you would be accepted in the Christian Community. If you like, I can contact a minister at an Evangelical Church here in the Sioux Falls."

He replied to his wife with some reluctance, "Sara, go ahead and do whatever it takes. However, it would be more beneficial if we were to become members of the largest congregation in the area."

Darrel thought to himself, "I'll be happy to be part of this unsophisticated group of potential investors."

It was not long before Methane Red Gas & Energy, LLC began receiving inquiries and investment money from local business people, farmers and ranchers. Sara's relatives had invested over fifty thousand dollars, collectively.

Finally, the co-conspirators had money to pay their bills and their vendors in South Dakota and Minnesota. Sara began receiving a salary while her husband chose not to have any documented income until he could settle his past financial troubles with the government.

After being in South Dakota for six months, the couple met the state's requirements for residency in order to avoid paying any Minnesota personal income taxes.

The couple returned to the Twin Cities on December 22 to spend the holidays with family and friends. Darrel went to see his daughters and grandkids while Sara joined her mother and kids and visited their many relatives in the Twin Cities.

Professor Daniel Alberding was given the go ahead to begin planning and building the manufacturing plant for gas converters in Brookings, SD. Emerson had convinced the City Council in Brookings to grant his business tax free land in the east side industrial park, provided MRGE would hire local college students for the manufacturing process.

Emerson was a shrewd executive working every angle possible; obtaining surreptitious ownership in everything he could. His parent holding company, Red Energy Development Industries (REDi), held all ownership stock secretly in Nevada. Sara did not know about the transfer of ownership nor would she have understood the legalities shielding Emerson from any tax liability.

He chartered a secret holding company in Nevada, legally, as a non profit organization allowing him to avoid filing corporate taxes or disclosing the names of the stockholders.

Darrel Emerson 'held all the cards' for his personal benefit. He could and would transfer assets and dollars in and out of MRGE without any questions from stockholders, the government or his third wife.

Sara only knew of the commissions and filing fees they were earning by selling the preferred stock in MRGE. The principle investment dollars were under Darrel's control and held in escrow in Nevada.

Finally, the couple could hire others to manage the business in SD so they could relax a little and enjoy life. They bought a five million dollar luxurious home on Lake Minnetonka in Minnesota. The mansion was on a private island with a private beach, an enclosed gazebo near the marina surrounded by thick woods and no neighbors nearby. This was Emerson's dream home, secretly owned by one of his shell corporations in Florida.

Soon after Sara and Darrel moved into their 18,000 square foot home, they joined an exclusive country club located across the lake; they bought new boats and expensive cars. They wanted everyone to know how wealthy they had become.

'A rags to riches story'.

Sara had always wanted to own a yacht on the St Croix River so Darrel bought a 40-foot Chris Craft and purchased a slip in an exclusive private marina south of Stillwater.

Even though Sara was still battling her ex-husband, Morgan Blake and his family in three states, she lost interest in fighting for her legally entitled marital assets. Her attorneys took over the court battles and kept Sara informed of their progress. She was determined to get some of the Blake family riches for her children's heritance. As the courts began seizing assets for child support arrearages, she would set aside the tainted money in a bank account specifically established for her kids' college education.

One Sunday morning while Sara and Darrel were enjoying the beautiful summer weather on their yacht named, R-IPO, Sara decided to ask some questions of her second husband.

"Darrel, how in the world will our investors get a return on the money they have entrusted with us?"

The executive paused for a moment and calmly answered her question while picking up a pen and a pad of notepaper. "Sara, why are you concerned? Methane Red Gas & Energy will soon begin manufacturing the gas converters in our South Dakota plant. The entire energy industry is anxiously awaiting the first demonstration of our patented electric generators and more and more investors are buying in before we establish the IPO. The preferred investor will get huge dividends when the IPO sells ten million shares over the counter, to the public, for $65 per share."

"Darrel, what if the technology doesn't work as hoped?" she pressed for more information.

"Then we hold off on demonstrating the invention until it does work. That is Professor Alberding's problem. We can hold off

Living in a Lie

doing an IPO for various reasons that preferred investors are use to. Sophisticated investors call that a *'Red Herring Portfolio.'* Meanwhile, your team needs to sell more investors."

Then Emerson informs his wife, "I'm traveling to Florida next week to research the possibility of opening another office near West Palm Beach. That is where the *'big money'* lives. I'll be staying at my daughter's beachfront town home. Susan is coming back to Minnesota to visit her sister for a while."

"Sara, I know you have plans to attend the five-day bible study in South Dakota next week. I'm not interested in interacting with those local church people. You enjoy that, so have a good time and take plenty of business cards." The arrogant capitalist instructed his submissive wife, "And say a prayer for my soul."

That afternoon, Captain Emerson and his *'third mate'* fired up the twin engines and piloted their precious yacht five miles up river to Stillwater. They tied up in a public slip and ventured into Pappy's Bar and Grill for cocktails. The bar was crowded so the two high school sweethearts sat on the patio deck watching the passing boats navigate under the Stillwater lift bridge.

Life was good. Sara was content. On the other hand, was it all a lie? Would her prosperity continue?

Chapter Seven

Unbelievable

July 3, 1993

IT WAS NINE AM WHEN I picked up my portable phone from the kitchen counter to hear Sara Blake's message left in my voice mail file. "Redmond, this is Sara Blake. I know you remember me with amorous thoughts. I need you to call me as soon as you get this message. I know you have caller ID so call me at the number listed. Keep this confidential."

I was surprised but pleased to hear from her after two years, "Sara, this is Red. How can I help you pretty lady?"

"Red, I need to hire your services to help me find out if my husband is loyal and trustworthy. I married him a year ago and life has been very rewarding for us with our new business venture. There is a lot of money at stake, millions of dollars and I need to know if he is being honest with me in our business dealings. I want you to find out if he is faithful to our marriage. I'll agree to pay your going rate for a week, plus expenses of course."

"Sara, of course I'll be happy to check him out and let you know the facts. Tell me more about the dude," I replied.

"Red, my husband is flying to Miami this afternoon. His daughter has a town house on the beach in West Palm Beach. This is where he'll be staying for the week. Before we hang up, I'll give you the address and his flight schedule. I want you to spy on him and record his appointments; any lunches or dinners; any social events and sleeping habits, if you know what I mean."

"Sara, can you fax me the info along with a photo of him? I'll give you my fax number. In order to carry this out, I'll need to rent a car, or maybe an Econo Van, or maybe both. I'll need to get a new high-powered lens for my camera. I assume you want photographs if I uncover any incriminating evidence. I need to stay in a nearby motel and charge you my daily rate of $1,000 per day, plus expenses. Is that okay with you?"

She responded with confidence, "Yes, by all means, Red. I just need to know what is going on while he is in Florida. I may need you to dig into his finances and check out our business financial statements. Something smells fishy and I have a gut feeling about our sudden prosperity."

"Ok, I'll get a flight to Miami tomorrow morning. I'll return in a week with my report and any evidence. I will not be calling you. I'll want at least $5,000 cash and the balance will be due five days later. Where would you like to meet?" I concluded.

"Red, I'll be in Sioux Falls that week and maybe we can meet at Crawford's Bar and Grill in downtown, on Phillips Avenue, between Tenth Street and Eleventh Street. How about lunch at one o'clock?" Sara instructed me.

"Certainly, charge me for traveling to Sioux Falls as well." She followed up her instructions, "I'll tell you more when we get together. Be safe."

––––––––––

I arrived in Miami around ten o'clock Tuesday morning and rented a dark red Chevy from the Redstar Car Rental Agency near the airport. The cabby loaded my baggage into the rental car's trunk as I placed my carry on bag in the front seat. I had packed all of my 'tools of the trade' for this caper including my handgun, just in case.

As I settled into the front seat, adjusting all the mirrors and steering wheel, I finally felt safe to look through the info and photos Sara faxed to me the day before. Unfortunately, I had quickly inserted the info into a brown manila envelope without examining it carefully. To my surprise, I was shocked to find out Sara's husband's name was 'Darrel Emerson', a client of mine from a few years ago.

"WOW," I declared aloud. "It's a small world. If I had known, I might have turned down the assignment. If I were an attorney, this caper might be a conflict of interest."

I convinced myself that it was ok to investigate Emerson now because his life must have changed over the years. I had an insignificant professional rule called a 'statute on limitations'. If Emerson is not supporting my business, I will not limit myself to work for others who will pay my fees.

The afternoon sun was setting in the western sky and I needed to locate the town house Emerson was staying in before finding a room for the night. After reviewing a local map that I found in the glove box, I was able to locate the address and drove to my destination before darkness. The town house was on North Ocean Boulevard overlooking the sandy beach of the Atlantic Ocean. After surveying the area, I realized how easy it would be to get on the sundeck after dark to observe any activity inside the home with its huge glass windows. The cool evening air would avert the occupants from coming outside. At least I would hope so.

I found an adequate motel room nearby and unpacked the car. I changed into my black turtleneck, jogging sweat pants and grabbed a black ski mask. I put my high-powered binoculars along with my camera and various high-powered lenses into my sports bag and then holstered my handgun under my left arm. All other valuables I packed into a suitcase and checked it with the night clerk in the lobby.

It was near ten o'clock in the evening when I parked a couple of blocks away and walked along the beach until reaching the town house.

After climbing the stairway from the beach, I perched myself behind a deck chair and table to hide my presence. It was not long before Darrel Emerson and his two guests appeared in the living room that over looked the panoramic view of the ocean.

The two black women were completely nude while embracing Emerson, who was naked. The Minnesota native was definitely a Scandinavian white boy. When the trio cuddled up in front of the gas fireplace, they looked like an ice cream sandwich melting away their passion.

I positioned my expensive camera on my tripod using a wide-angle lens to capture the architecture of the town house from the far end of the deck. Then I thought to myself, "Why am I doing this? I need to move in closer and use my telephoto lens." The scene was steamy and sultry as I used the sequential shutter capturing every moment of Emerson's pleasure. "WOW."

I could have stayed for hours watching the ardent circus; however, I did get dozens of great photos to confirm Sara's suspicion. Her husband was without a doubt a scoundrel.

I left the scene of decadence around midnight after taking pictures of the cars near the rear of the house. I knew I would be observing Emerson the next day so I returned to my motel room for needed sleep. If Emerson had business in Florida, I would be following him to find out what he was up to. I already knew what kind of snake he was. I just had to prove it to Sara.

The second night while watching the beach house, Emerson entertained (me from afar) and a very beautiful red-haired woman in front of the fireplace. I took more photos and left earlier than the night before.

After two nights and three days, I left West Palm Beach with a suitcase full of incriminating evidence that would convince a blind jury of Emerson's infidelity. I had observed him as he visited three different banks and a law firm that had offices in Asia. I was certain he was covering his tracks and moving money out of his sleazy investments.

I had a profound dislike for this immoral and scandalous executive who was deceiving the world. He was playing the game of self-indulgence, by himself for himself while collaborating with the devil himself.

I left the Twin Cities in the early morning on July 12, in anticipation of the four hour drive to Sioux Falls. I was meeting Sara at one o'clock and wanted to be there early to check out the surrounding area. I wondered why Sara was in a city in the middle of nowhere. South Dakota is a State without many cities, not many lakes or rivers, mainly flat farmland with corn fields, alfalfa fields and cattle ranches.

The last time I saw Sara was over two years ago.

When she entered the historical bar and grill, all eyes noticed her promenade; her expensive executive clothing; her stylish figure and youthful complexion topped off with flowing long brown hair underneath a large summer hat.

She looked quite sophisticated and wealthy, a great deal different from when she was an executive recruiter. I could tell by the smell of her perfume, she bought only the best and most expensive.

I thought to myself, "Good show, Sara! No one would ever believe you were a former Baptist minister's wife from rural Illinois. If the women of Freedom could see you now, they would try to escape their own dreadful fate."

I was the proud knight that set her free to live life on her terms. Now, a couple of years later, I was only a meager soldier for her majesty, the queen. It was amazing to see how money changed this submissive soul. No longer was Sara a modest woman, afraid to be assertive or self-centered. Now, she dominated anyone and everyone who might approach her.

"Sara, it is good to see you. It has been about two years, right? Tell me how life has been and why you are here in South Dakota," as I greeted her with a kiss and a hug.

As she slid into the private booth, I noticed her manicured polished nails as she replied, "Red, I've been good. Life is good. God has blessed me with a new business and a better man then Morgan Blake. I'm still in court fighting for my marital assets, child

Living in a Lie

support and parental rights. Morgan was able to get supervised visitation through the county. My kids do not want any part of their father and his religious preaching but they have to endure his madness for now."

"How about you? Any exciting capers? Any other damsels in distress?" she teased me with a smile.

"Well, Sara. The escapade you sent me on has had plenty of intrigue and mystery. It so happens, I met Mr. Emerson years ago. He employed me many times in the 80's and most recently in 1990. Now, I cannot divulge any confidential or privileged details but I have to say, he is not the man you think his is," I replied with caution.

"Oh, Red, I know you are a little jealous of my hero. My husband is a wise and intelligent executive who has the ability to make a lot of money in the venture capital business," she responded with a laugh in her voice.

"Matter of fact, since we've been married, our net worth has grown to be more than fifty million dollars, as best I can determine. We have a huge house on an island in Lake Minnetonka, a yacht on the St Croix River, a condo in Mexico and recently we started building a beautiful cabin/lodge in Northern Minnesota, near Cross Lake," Sara explained cheerfully.

"Just the other day, Darrel gave me this beautiful pearl necklace as an anniversary gift. He is a wonderful man and treats me well," she continued to justify her new way of life. "Our new business venture, Methane Red Gas & Energy will become a revolutionary invention manufactured in Brookings. Darrel expects our patented device will soon be ready for distribution worldwide."

"Oh, really," I replied with a questionable tone to my voice. "Did you know he has done something like this before?"

"Yes," she replied. "He told me he made millions on an invention called the Red Rover."

"Oh, really !!!" I responded with interest. "Did he use his own money to start up this venture in South Dakota?"

"No, we raised millions of dollars through our venture capital business by selling preferred stock to wealthy cattle ranchers from around here, in North Dakota, Iowa, Montana, Nebraska and Minnesota. My relatives got a 10% return on their investment within the first year," Sara explained with a blissful tone in her voice.

She continued telling her exciting news, "In less than a year, I personally recruited over one hundred investors who purchased ten million shares each, in order to qualify. Red, do you know how much money that totals?"

I humbly responded, "Yes, Sara, I figure that is more than one hundred million dollars. No doubt you get the filing fees, registration fees and a percentage of their capital gains."

"Oh yes, yes. I have a staff of investment brokers here in Sioux Falls and in our office near our home in Wayzata," she revealed. "Darrel is so smart with our earnings and our personal investments that we will be rich for the rest of our lives. In addition, the best thing of all, he loves me as I've always wanted to be loved. I trust him. I believe in him and I know he'll be there for me, even if I lose my youthful appearance and age a little."

It was hard for me to restrain myself knowing what I uncovered in my investigation in Florida. Again I express my surprise, "Oh, really. Are you sure everything is for real?"

"Yes, Red. God has answered my prayers and has blessed my life. I have so many good friends at the church I attend here in Sioux Falls. Moreover, my family in Minnesota is happy for me. They all enjoy coming to my home on Lake Minnetonka for holidays and family functions."

I had to caution her before I expose the truth about her adulterous husband. "Sara, please take a few minutes and come back to earth. Darrel Emerson has many enemies and the government is watching him. His many investment schemes have failed in the past, hurting hundreds of investors. I can only imagine the SEC and the Justice Department are looking into all of his unsuccessful investment portfolios. If he is caught conducting illegal investment transactions and avoiding US Federal Taxes, he will go to jail and you may be a co-conspirator."

"Let me ask you, Sara. Who is the CEO of your Venture Capital Bank?" I inquired curiously.

Sara replied to my inquest, "I am but Darrell wanted me to have sole ownership in our business to protect my investment and my families' investment. He said 'I would be in control of my destiny no matter what happens to him.' He assured me I could not be held accountable to his past. If the IRS brought charges against him for his past business failures, I could claim 'Injured Spouse' and file my taxes separately and not be held liable for his mistakes."

I responded carefully not to cause panic, "Sara, did you seek the advice of an attorney before starting this joint venture with your husband? Is Darrel a part owner? Can he access the business bank accounts without your approval? Does your business have a Certified Public Accountant who reviews the business financials every quarter and files year end taxes? Are there other stockholders or a board of directors involved in the business?"

She laughed while answering, "Redmond, you are so paranoid. I trust my husband completely. He said he would take care of all the legalities to protect my interests and protect me from any tax liability issues. Darrel is very knowledgeable of all the legal details. He could be an attorney if he took the bar examine."

"Redmond, enough of that suspicious talk. I probably should not have told you any of my private business. What did you find out while in Florida?" she finally asked.

"Sara, before I give you my report, I have to ask if you can pay my fees and expenses at this point. The good news is, I only need to charge you for four days, my costs of round trip airline tickets, one auto rental, three nights and expenses... instead of five nights. Instead of the estimated ten thousand dollars, I'll charge you six grand. I prefer cash. Can you pay that now?"

"Redmond, of course I can and I'll even buy lunch," she replied with a confident smile on her face. "Here is six thousand dollars and an additional five hundred for your time in meeting me here today," she replies while passing the envelope under the table. "Tell me what my husband is up to in West Palm Beach. I'm anxious to know if he is going to surprise me with another house or a new office or more expensive jewelry."

"Sara, I watched him at the beachfront condo Tuesday and Wednesday nights without him knowing. I followed him to and from one bank and then to another bank located in an office building on Wednesday and Thursday. I know for sure he's not buying any property in his name in Florida. He did not stop at any jewelry store. I did check with one of my confidential contacts in the Justice Department in Miami and they are looking for Darrel Emerson. The Feds are searching tax records and property records nationwide. They have an order to apprehend him if he uses his passport. His investors from the past five years have filed a class action suit seeking retribution for their losses in his many schemes. The IRS is searching for him with regards to millions of dollars in unpaid taxes," as I itemized my findings for her.

"Sara, Darrel Emerson is not who you think he is. What he has disclosed to you is only the tip of a huge pyramid of fraud and swindles that exceed over a billion dollars," I cautiously explained to her.

I continued to report all my discovery information about Emerson's financial dealings. "The Feds are looking into the Red Rover Project, Redstone Venture Capital Investments, Redwood Industries, Red Earth Properties and a recent start up holding company in Las Vegas called Red Energy Development Industries. That last one (REDi), his daughter is listed as the CEO and sole stockholder. My sources tell me he has over one hundred million dollars in deposits held in escrow for Methane Red Gas & Energy, which has a corporate office here in Sioux Falls."

Finally, with all the information I shared with her, she looked concerned and responded with a couple of questions. "Red, how can I protect myself? What should I do?"

"Sara, it might be best to seek council. I'm not a licensed attorney, as you know. However, you need to separate your finances from his. You need to obtain documents that will shelter you from his shady investment schemes. You need to exempt yourself from his legal problems and any back taxes that he owes," I instructed her.

"Is your name on any mortgages, automobile titles, boats titles or joint bank accounts?" I quickly asked her. "Who is the CEO and major stockholder in the business here in South Dakota?"

With a worried look on her face she answered, "I am the CEO and the only original stockholder. Darrel is in charge of the financials and money management."

With concern, I responded, "Sara, the way I see things... if this new Methane Gas Converter does not work, you will lose everything and Emerson has control of the invested principle in Las Vegas. You are the one who will be charged with fraud, dishonesty and larceny. You will be the one held accountable for repaying all fees and commissions you took from selling stock to investors. Unless you have a license to sell stock, you and all your sales associates will be prosecuted for violating SEC Rules and Federal Laws. Because you accepted the responsibilities of CEO, the burden falls on you. There is a legal doctrine called 'Implied Admissions' or 'Admission of Interests' that holds a CEO accountable to the law, stockholders and the IRS."

I concluded my dissertation by saying, "Quite frankly my dear, you are in deep trouble. Emerson has conned you into taking the fall while he controls the money. Even if you were to divorce him, you are solely responsible for the Investment Firm here in Sioux Falls."

She started crying while pleading for more advice. "Red, what can I do? I cannot ask Darrel to help me. He'll get suspicious and ask why I am concerned. Tell me my dear friend... what must I do to avoid losing all my money and my families' money?"

"If you divorce him, he'll blame you and your inexperience in business. Who knows what he might do? When he is found and then prosecuted in Federal Court, you could be charged as an accomplice in his current unlawful businesses," I responded with concern.

"The only option you have to avoid prosecution is killing him," I commented with a smile. "Sara, you know I'm just kidding. However, if he is dead <u>he</u> cannot testify for or against you. You could simply state your naivety and let the government prove otherwise. Without Darrel Emerson to testify, you may be able to convince a jury of your innocence under the 'clean hands' doctrine. If you had no idea of what was illegal or against SEC Rules, the only thing you would be guilty of would be following your husband's directives."

The sophisticated looking business woman sat quite still for a few minutes while I finished my hamburger and beverage. The food was good and the beer quenched my thirst. I could see her carefully calculating her options without disclosing her thoughts. She did not lose her composure or confidence while analyzing my suggestions and advice.

Sara replied, "Red, I will take your advice under advisement with great concern. Is there anything else I should know before we part?"

"Yes, there is something else you should know," I reluctantly responded. "Your husband is not faithful to you. He is guilty of many transgressions. I have some photos for you to review if you want proof."

The faithful Christian wife quickly interrupted my presentation. "Red, I know I have been living in a lie. There were many women before me and there have been others since we were married. My husband is a philanderer with an open fly. You only verified my suspicions. Thank you. I need no further proof. Mr. Emerson will soon lose his hunting license so help me God."

It must have been four o'clock in the afternoon when I drove away from the old restaurant leaving Sara standing in the parking lot near her new Jaguar. She was without emotion looking very subdued... maybe near tears. She was a strong diva determined to corner her husband in his lies before he loses their fortune to the Feds.

I headed east on I-80 towards Minnesota. It would be a long drive with a lot to think about. I was feeling sad for Sara. Again, her dreams of being wealthy had ended because of her husband's lies and deceit. She had the best intentions to live a successful life with all of God's benevolence. She wanted to become a pillar of her newfound church, exhibiting her Christian beliefs by helping battered women who are abandoned in their marriages.

Maybe, after this massive episode in her disappointing life, she might be able to restore her lifetime dream. I sort of felt she could pick herself up again and praise God for giving her strength to move on.

Again, Sara would have to face adversity to have her freedom. She would be able to escape and survive the avalanche of financial and legal ruin that would devastate her business and wealthy lifestyle. Her marriage might be over but Sara was not finished.

Nearing Albert Lea I headed north on 35W, my thoughts were fading away as my cell phone began ringing. I picked up the phone and heard a voice from the past, "Redmond is that you? I've been trying to contact you all day."

"Hello, yes this is Redmond Herring. Who's calling me?" I responded with hesitation.

"Herring, this is Darrel Emerson. Do you remember me from a couple of years ago? I have a big job for you. Can we meet soon?"

"Sure, what is this about? Where are you now?" I replied with caution after spending the afternoon with his wife.

"Herring, I might be in trouble with the Feds and they may have tapped my phones so let me be quick. Can you meet some place safe in the morning?"

My thoughts were in a maze. My thinking became confused. Were the Feds listening now? Would I be implicated and connected to their investigation of Emerson? I now wondered if Sara had a wire and recorded me for the Feds? Were they closing in on my unsavory past and me? Was Emerson set up to catch me? How would I know whom to trust, anymore?

"Hey, Emerson, let's not talk on the phone anymore. As your legal council, we need to meet in private. Let's meet at your favorite restaurant in St. Paul at noon tomorrow. Ok?" I responded hoping to scare the Feds away if they were listening. Attorney client privilege is more sacred then anyone's 'Rights to Privacy.' I know judges will penalize any government agent that violates my private conversations with any client.

"Ok, I'll be there. Thanks, buddy," the voice hung up and my phone went silent.

Whew... I asked myself, how in the world did I get into the middle of this mess. Damn. Life was rather mundane and peaceful

Living in a Lie

until now. It is the curse of 'Sara.' Why did I see her again and then agree to help her?

I tried to dismiss all my past illegal activities that could incarcerate me for the rest of my life. I could make up an alias and change my name, sell everything, cash in my fortune and move to Australia to live among those English criminals that took refuge on that continent a hundred years ago. Sure, that is what I will do. I could change my name to 'Stupid Idiot'. Damn.

Chapter Eight

False Pretense

THE CAROUSEL RESTAURANT WAS LOCATED at the top of the Radisson Hotel in downtown St. Paul attached to a secluded parking ramp used mainly by the patrons of the hotel. During the weekends, the revolving nightclub provided entertainment with a string quartet for the evening diners.

This was a great spot for our semi-private luncheon with Emerson. The fancy club had white linen tablecloths, real silverware, the best wines and was located on the 22nd floor above Wabasha Street which overlooked the Mississippi River. We could sit and talk for as long as needed without the wait staff nudging us to finish. As far as I could tell, the staff was not familiar with me. However, I was hoping Emerson would be anonymous.

I arrived fifteen minutes early as I always do and asked for a table far away from the other customers. I instructed the assigned server to be as inconspicuous as possible and not to interrupt. She acknowledged my request and pledged her service with cooperation.

Precisely at high noon, Darrel Emerson stepped out of the elevator with the charisma of a wealthy, successful businessman expecting personal attention from the maitre d'. He was escorted to my table; we shook hands, greeted each other and then sat looking out over the panoramic skyline.

I never forgot how much Emerson liked the Carousel for the food but mostly for the view. He enjoyed looking down on the working class people who had real jobs earning meager wages and paying excessive income taxes on their employment. This 'small town' guy had swindled his way to the top of society, without any apology, to became a rich arrogant snob.

As we glanced over the menu, I took notice of this sophisticated criminal sitting next to me in the finest clothing money could buy. He wore an open button-down collar, white on white silk shirt with his initials monogrammed on the sleeves, 'DJE.'

His camel colored silk dress pants complimented his Italian leather shoes. His leather belt cost more then the finest wine in the restaurant. He had a gold Rolex watch on his left arm and a gold bracelet on his right arm.

Darrel Emerson's curly blonde hair was turning gray and he was looking stressed out. No doubt, he was always 'looking over his shoulder' day and night. I could only imagine how difficult it was for him to be on guard everywhere while avoiding the authorities.

The last time we were together, he employed me to conceal and transport twenty-five million dollars in cash to be deposited into his nine secret bank accounts in the Cayman Islands. It seemed to me, that he was always moving huge amounts of cash to his offshore bank accounts. I have no idea why he trusted me. Over the past ten years, I followed his instructions and accomplished my objectives without any problems for my client or for me.

He did pay me well to be his trusted confidant.

Even though I had recently investigated his covert activities for his wife, Emerson had no reason to have misgivings about me. I did what he wanted and kept my mouth shut.

After the server took our orders, Emerson spoke quietly while looking directly into my eyes, "Redmond, I really need your help. I'm in serious trouble with the government and there are many angry investors whom are trying to incarcerate me, maybe even kill me. I have a plan and need you to follow my instructions precisely without any hesitation, whatsoever."

"I'm listening," as I affirmed his directives.

"As you know, I have managed to stash a few bucks away into nine numbered bank accounts in the Cayman Islands, for my retirement of course. All of my speculative ventures have purposely failed and those investors who were involved have lost their initial investments, blaming me for their losses."

Living in a Lie

"A few years ago, I married my high school sweetheart who has recently uncovered my fraudulent investment schemes and now wants a divorce. She has threatened to divulge all my business holdings and secret enterprises to the authorities if I do not pay her twenty million in cash and agree to a divorce," Emerson was pleading his case to me, his only friend.

"Ok," I responded with hesitation wondering why his plight should involve me.

"Redmond, I've thought a lot about all my misdeeds and all my misfortunes. The best thing I can do for my wife, Sara, and my daughters will be to die a sudden unexpected death. Sara has an insurance policy on my life for five hundred thousand, which should be enough to hire attorneys to sort out our finances, liquidate our assets and pay our joint marital taxes. The government will have to figure out what I owe in back taxes and where all the money went that was paid to me. Most of my past investors will not tell the truth to the authorities because they will be subjected to unrelenting IRS audits for tax evasion. Sara will be able to claim 'Injured Spouse' and seek relief from any liabilities that occurred before we were married."

"Ok, what about any ventures you and Sara started while you married?" I inquired carefully.

"The most important piece of my plan is Sara. She is a very smart business woman with many important friends in the church she attends in Sioux Falls. I'm sure she'll be able to sort out the details of our business venture, Methane Red Gas and Energy, which should make her a very wealthy woman."

Emerson began showing some emotions but continued explaining his own death, "With me gone, Sara can take over the business bank accounts in Vegas and pay off any investors that want out and then sell our patent rights and invention copyrights to the inventor who can then form a new group of investors that will take over."

"Ok, where do I come into this plan of yours?" I asked, not wanting any part of Emerson's concocted schemes.

The shrewd criminal recited his instructions, "I want you to charter a jet out of Miami and fly to Cayman Islands for a day. I will inform the banks by special messenger that you are flying to the islands to withdraw all my funds. Each bank will receive detailed instructions on how to transfer the containers of cash to you. Because of the large amount of cash, you'll have to make nine separate withdrawals and each case will then be handed over to one of eight special couriers that will fly to various destinations around the world. As you pick up each container, you will meet each courier in a separate airport hanger. Each of the couriers will have instructions where to fly and where to deposit my money. No one will know the eight destinations except for me."

Emerson continued his instructions, "The ninth and final withdrawal of cash is yours to do with whatever you decide. This is your reward for being a confidant and loyal friend for the past ten years. I have trusted you to deposit over one hundred million

Living in a Lie

dollars in those nine accounts. Inside the last container will also be a briefcase with a million dollars inside. Please bring that cash to me. When you return from your assignment, do not call me. I know the feds are closing in and may be listening to my calls and watching my homes."

With great surprise I responded, "Mr. Emerson... I thank you for trusting me and for your generosity. When do you want me to accomplish this?"

"I want you to arrive at the airport, in the Cayman Islands, on September 6, Labor Day. The banks will be open because the islands do not celebrate Labor Day as a holiday."

He continued as I took brief notes, "After you return to Minnesota, you are to drive south on 35W towards Faribault on September 10th. As you near Faribault, there will be an exit for Highway 60. Take 60 west towards Waterville. About two miles from that exit, you will see Cannon Lake on your right side. Look for a beach and a park called 'Shager Park.' Pull in there. You'll see a small grove of saplings and tall grass directly left or west of the sign, near the beach front and the lake. In the grove of trees, I want you to partially bury that briefcase wrapped in a black garbage bag. Leave a small corner of the bag sticking out above the dirt and rocks. I'll be stopping at the spot during the early evening hours to retrieve the money."

"No matter what happens just remember what I'm saying... I'm always very precise in my plans. We will never see each other again. Thank you my good and faithful servant. Enjoy your new found wealth," Emerson concluded our meeting.

As we shook hands, he said, "Redmond, you might want to search out my wife, Sara. She will need your expertise in the months ahead straightening out my mess. You might find her quite appealing."

I waited a few days before contacting Sara Blake-Emerson before telephoning her office in Minnesota. Her very polite receptionist answered. She put me on hold for a brief moment and then forwarded my call to her employer.

"Redmond, it's a delight to hear from you. I thought our business was over. How can I help you?" Sara's voice was firm but not loud.

"Sara, I have some great news for you which will improve your future concerns. We need to meet in private as soon as you can," I replied with caution anticipating the Feds were listening in nearby.

"Ok Redmond, what do you suggest?" she responded.

"Sara, remember where we first had lunch. Where we met for the first time? Meet me there at one o'clock on Monday. Do not tell anyone about our meeting," I spoke slowly and carefully.

"I'll look forward to seeing you then," she hung up.

Living in a Lie

I arrive at the Pantry in Edenborough fifteen minutes before my meeting and sat in the parking lot watching the customers leaving the secluded restaurant. I did not see any government vehicles or FBI sedans, those Ford Crown Victoria's that were widely used by the US Government.

I waited patiently until Sara arrived in her Jaguar and then I greeted her near the front entrance to her surprise. "Sara, thanks for meeting me. We have to be very careful. I think the Feds are tracking you and Darrel. They are listening in on your phones and possibly have 'bugs' in your offices. They may have followed you here so be careful as we talk."

"Redmond, it's good to see you again. I'll speak with caution. Remember that cold January day when we first met here? So much has happened. I was so naive and dirt poor with no idea of what to expect in my struggle to escape from my husband, Morgan, and from that old farm in Freedom, Illinois," Sara spoke with reticence.

The host guided us towards a private booth near the back windows away from other customers. We were handed large luncheon menus as the server filled our glasses with water.

"Sara, you look wonderful today. Your black and white sweater blouse compliments your dark hair. I see you are wearing that pearl necklace again. Are your matching earrings new?" I started our conversation slowly not knowing if Sara was recording our meeting.

"Redmond, lets cut the crap. What's so important that brings us together again?" she insisted on moving things along while ignoring any adoration.

"It is Darrel. He does not know about our history. He has hired me to move some of his assets in fear of the authorities finding them. I think he is getting ready to disappear leaving you with big problems," I summarized my concerns knowing the Feds could be listening or Sara was taping me.

"That's interesting," she replied. "When do you think he will make his move?"

"Maybe in the next few months," I was vague in my answer for many reasons.

"Based on all of your other suspicions, I'll have to think about my options before I do anything," this coy sophisticated woman replied.

I encouraged her to take my advice, "Sara, Darrel is not the man you think he is. Beware of what can happen if he feels trapped by his own circumstances. His past is catching up to him and you must protect yourself first."

"Ok, Redmond lets relax and reminisce about our past," she suggested as she flipped her hair off to the side. "Are you interested in getting back together if Darrel disappears?"

"Sara, I'll answer that question some other time," I deflected her tease.

Living in a Lie

September 1993...

I did my job precisely as Emerson instructed and returned to Minnesota with a large cache to hide away in a bank box before going home. I took a few minutes to unpack, sort through my mail and open a bottle of merlot before settling in to rewind my voice message machine. There were eight messages waiting to be replayed; five were unimportant. To my surprise, Sara Emerson had called three times with very disturbing news.

"Redmond, please call me as soon as you can," Sara's voice sounded concerned.

"Redmond, please pick up if you are there," Sara insisted with a forceful voice.

"Redmond, please call me when you get this message. Darrel has had an accident and he is dead. His funeral is on Saturday, September 11. His viewing will be on Friday evening starting at five o'clock in Waterville at the Emerson Funeral Home. Please call me," Sara was crying as she recorded the sad news of her husband's death.

"Wow," I spoke aloud in response to the unexpected news. What has happened... did Sara kill him? Did some angry investor find him and assassinate the big swindler? I started asking myself so many questions it was hard to comprehend my next move.

I collected my thoughts and then finally called Sara. "Sara, this is Redmond. I got your message. Tell me what has happened. How did Darrel die? How can I help you?"

"Redmond, Darrel was fishing with a cousin on Sakatah Lake yesterday, when their boat capsized spilling them into the water. Darrel was found floating facedown near the north shoreline and his body was taken to the local funeral home which is also the Southern Le Sueur County's morgue. The funeral director determined the cause of death was cardiac arrest. Darrel had a heart attack while trying to swim to shore. He's gone, Red. I'm so sad. His family in Waterville made all the arrangements which I'm grateful for. The funeral service will be on Saturday at ten in the morning. Can you be there for me?"

I replied to her, "Sara, of course I'll be there at the viewing and again at his funeral on Saturday. I guess I'll stay in Faribault at the Galaxy Motor Inn. How about you? Shall we meet for a drink on Friday evening?"

"Oh, Redmond, thank you. You are always there for me when I need comforting. Maybe we could drive to Waterville together on Friday afternoon," she suggested.

"Sara, I can't do that. I have a business luncheon in Mankato and will be driving to Waterville afterwards. I'll see you at the funeral home. I'm very sorry for your loss. I know you loved your husband and he loved you," I replied anticipating that the Feds were listening to our conversation.

Living in a Lie

Friday morning was calm and warm for September. However, I could feel the atmosphere changing to fall. I drove south to Faribault and noticed the sumac along the highway turning red and the tall grass was browning.

I took the exit off Interstate 35W to get on Highway 60 that would take me to Waterville. Two miles later, I was looking for the park near Cannon Lake. Emerson's instructions were accurate and precise as I pulled into the park. There was the sign he mentioned and I noticed the grove of trees near the beach. I parked my car to block the view of the area where I would bury the secret briefcase full of money. I found a plentiful supply of large rocks to cover the stash leaving a small edge of the garbage bag sticking out per Emerson's instructions.

I felt his idea was rather risky, leaving a million dollars where others could possibly find it. However, that is what my employer wanted.

While driving away, I noticed the cool lake water looked bluer than normal and the river birch leaves were turning yellow. The wind was calm and the afternoon temperatures were nearing seventy degrees.

I was still in a state of shock thinking that Emerson was dead and would be buried tomorrow. The day seemed surreal. I'm driving to Emerson's wake on the exact day he wanted me to bury the money along the exact highway that takes me to Waterville where he died two days ago; after all his secret offshore assets were distributed around the world, four days ago.

If I had not taken notes when I last met with Emerson in St. Paul a couple of months ago, I would not believe what was happening. I tore those notes into small pieces and disposed the small particles of evidence out the window while driving down the roadway.

I reminded myself, 'Someday, I need to write a book about all this. No one will believe it.'

I continued my drive to Emerson's deathbed.

———————

Waterville is located at the southwestern end of Sakatah Lake, which is on the southern border of Le Sueur County, seventy miles south of the Twin Cities in the middle of Southern Minnesota. There are small towns and hundreds of lakes in the fertile farm country where immigrants migrated from Europe over a hundred years ago.

As pioneers settled the land, they established European traditions and Christian religions. Mainly Catholics, Lutherans and Baptists live in the country while the Jewish were merchants who built cities along the Minnesota and Mississippi rivers for shipping.

Waterville descendants were mainly Catholics and Lutherans with a small congregation of Baptists in town. Darrel Emerson's ancestors were grain farmers with some livestock while Sara Harrison's family started a fishing and boat rental business on the Sakatah Lake and were Baptist.

Darrel Emerson and his family are highly respected Catholics supporting the community and the church for decades. Darrel graduated from high school in 1967 as valedictorian. He lettered in basketball, tennis and golf. He left his hometown to attend Mankato State College to get his BA in business graduating in 1971.

From college, he started his career in banking and finance by taking a low level internship with an investment bank in the Twin Cities. After working in minimum salary jobs for eight years, he took a risk and started his own business called Redstone Venture Capital, soliciting hundreds of wealthy investors to invest in his startup venture called Red Rover, a gold extracting machine.

He made over a million dollars in less than a year and went on to become a multi-millionaire and eventually a billionaire within fifteen years. He had a taste for money and wanted to become a very wealthy man. However, he did fleece millions of dollars from his investors without any hesitation or guilt.

Darrel Emerson always told his investors, "If you cannot afford to risk your money, then do not use it." That was his way of justifying his frauds and schemes. "The very wealthy need losses to offset their gains for tax deductions and I'll be happy to provide them with the means of doing that."

Darrel never forgot his roots or his heritage, returning to Southern Minnesota annually. He was generous with his fortune buying expensive gifts for his relatives and friends. Darrel once bought his high school friend a ten thousand dollar fishing boat with a motor and trailer which he would use when he returned to his home.

The Emerson clan lived throughout the river valley and in surrounding counties. They were farmers, merchants, lawyers, a priest and a mortician who owned the only mortuary in town, who was explicitly the only county coroner in the area.

Years ago, Darrel had purchased a large parcel of land in the local Catholic cemetery for his last remains and for all of his relatives who wanted to be near their ancestors.

Darrel Emerson had wanted to be buried in the family plot which was just down the road from the family farm.

Everyone who knew the successful businessman would attend his funeral on Saturday. The afternoon before, anyone could come by the funeral home for viewing the town's favorite son. The local mayor ordered all flags to be on display, at half-mast over the weekend, in honor of Darrel James Emerson.

The locals did not know Darrel as I did. His current wife, Sara Harrison-Blake-Emerson, would be _very_ present at this somber event.

I arrived at the funeral home at five-thirty to find a line of friends and relatives waiting to pay their last respects. There must have been at least a hundred people wanting to say goodbye to Darrel Emerson.

It was not long before Sara found me and escorted me inside as she introduced me to relatives as Emerson's 'longtime business partner.' I thought to myself, "Ya, sure, his partner in his many crimes."

I whispered in her ear, "We need to talk tonight. The Feds are here waiting to see if Darrel is dead. I can't believe he's gone. Did you have something to do with this, Sara?"

She glared at me with distain, "Redmond, I would never think of such a thing. I married my high school sweetheart with a promise to God... until death do we part."

"I loved him with all my heart giving him the best years of my life," the vixen clarified herself as we walked near the open casket seeing her husband's body.

I suddenly grab Sara's arm while looking at her deceased husband, "Sara, he doesn't look dead. I think his throat muscles are flinching. Look carefully."

She looked at Emerson and then at me and then at Darrel's uncle, the mortician, and walked away with her hand covering her mouth. At that point, Sara knew that Darrel Emerson was pulling off his greatest scam ever. No doubt, he was planning to leave her, take his money and run from prosecution for all of his crimes.

I should have figured him out before this revealing moment. Emerson was a master conspirator and his last hoax will set him free to live a life in luxury far away from the US Government wherever that might be.

I thought to myself, "This is unbelievable." I'll stand back and watch how this story unfolds. I can see that Sara is angry as she exits the viewing area to spend a few minutes in her silver Jaguar crying out her emotions.

I approached her as she rolled down the window and spoke quietly to me, "Redmond, I'll see you in Faribault at the Lavender Inn at eight o'clock tonight. I do not have a motel room or any plans for the night. Will you comfort me?"

I reluctantly answered, "Yes, I'll see you later."

Saturday morning came earlier then normal with Sara cuddled up in my arms. She moved slightly as I got up to prepare for the day by taking a shower.

It wasn't long before she joined me as she began washing my back. I turned to face her, admiring this voluptuous woman as I took the soapy washcloth from her and began washing her breast. After our amorous night together, I was hoping she wanted more passion from me.

She reminded me of her pressing timeline for this ceremonial day. She needed to be in Waterville by nine o'clock while I could linger behind for thirty minutes.

I encouraged her to take over the bathroom as I watched her promenade around the hotel room in her lingerie. She hurried while putting on a black silk blouse with an all black pleated skirt, which covered her gorgeous legs down to her knees.

Living in a Lie

She wore dark hosiery with black satin high heels and a gold ankle bracelet. She had a small black purse and carried along a pair of long black gloves. After putting on an expensive pearl necklace, she brushed her black hair back to fasten her pierced pearl earrings.

Before kissing me goodbye, she sprayed expensive perfume on her hair, body and hands grabbing her wide brim black summer hat.

It was hard to let her go. I wanted to spend the day between the sheets; however, we were both anxious to return to Waterville to witness her husband's grand finale.

Sara opened the door to leave the motel room expressing her concerns, "Redmond, Darrel Emerson is not going to get away with his exit plan. The Feds will catch him."

Saturday, September 11, 1993, 9:30 AM

On the way from Faribault to Waterville, I decide to stop by the drop site to check on Emerson's cache. To my surprise, but relieved, the garbage bag and contents were gone without a trace. I was hopeful the intended benefactor had snatched the money up.

As I arrived at the church parking lot near the funeral home, there was a lot of activity at the side door of the building. Sara was directing the funeral workers to get her husband's coffin in the church quickly. I could hear her telling the mortician that flowers needed to be put on the closed casket and placed on the pedestal tables nearby for the Requiem Mass.

People were arriving as the priest greeted the mourners at the main entry. I scanned the parking lot looking for anyone I might know and then noticed a black sedan parked curbside across from the church. The federal agents were present. I stayed in my car until the church doors were closed and everyone was inside.

After entering, I sat in the back pew watching the details unfold for this sacred Catholic ritual. Typically, the viewing or visitation was the day before the funeral with an open casket. The day of the funeral, the mortician closed and locked the coffin before moving it into the church. No one, not even family could view the deceased before the burial.

I felt a sense of remorse knowing I would never see Darrel Emerson ever again. He was my best client paying me more than two million dollars over the past ten years. I suppose I was his only confidant.

As the church bells rang, the entire town of one thousand knew of the Emerson family's loss. The Saturday morning AM mass began on time at ten o'clock, as the organist blasted out a thundering refrain that shook the large stained glass windows on all sides. The choir stood as the priest gestured the congregation to do the same.

Living in a Lie

I could see Sara standing in the front row near the Emerson family. Worshippers filled the old-fashioned cathedral with a few latecomers standing in the back foyer.

The Requiem Mass was emotional as the priest gave homage to the man whom he baptized as a child, to the boy that he confirmed as a teenager, to the adult that he married in the church in 1972.

Darrel's father stood near his son's casket and told the audience how proud the Emerson family was of their hero. He told the audiences of his son's lifetime accomplishments as the Federal Marshals quietly watch from the back entry.

The mass took about an hour.

After a prayer was recited, the parade of sadness started with Emerson's four brothers carrying the golden casket down the center aisle towards the back. A procession lead by family and friends left their pews crying and weeping as the congregation waited for their dismissal by the ushers.

That is when I saw Emerson's previous partner, Tyler Castor, step out from the third row of pews to become part of the grieving pageant. She wore a black business suit with a large black summer hat covering part of her face.

I thought to myself as I observed her peaceful presence, "Wow, talk about the past coming to visit the present."

When I finally walked out of the church, I spotted the stunning blonde standing by herself watching as Emerson's body was lifted into the hearse. She quickly kissed the casket and walked away.

That is when I walked over and introduced myself to the sophisticated woman, "Tyler Castor, you do not know me but I was a confidant to Darrel Emerson during his years in Las Vegas. He spoke highly of you and was saddened when you left his business and married. Are you still living in the Twin Cities?"

She seemed surprised that anyone knew her but was relieved to be talking to someone. I suggested she ride with me to the cemetery and we could talk in private. She accepted my invitation without hesitation.

It was not long before the mortician and the County Sheriff had the motorcade organized and moving along.

As Tyler settled into my car, I broke the silence by asking, "Tyler, how long has it been since you and Darrel talked?"

She replied carefully not knowing a lot about me, "Well, a few months ago Darrel contacted me and asked me and my husband if we might be interested in purchasing his cabin in Northern Minnesota near Cross Lake. It so happens we were looking. He said he would give us a good deal, if we could buy the 10,000 square foot log cabin structure for cash. It was brand new, just finished and valued at three million. He was willing to let it go for one million if we purchased the property this summer."

The wealthy woman continued, "We did look at it and we did purchase the lake home when Emerson included the boats and pontoon. It was just two week ago he signed over the title and took our money. We really got a good buy."

Living in a Lie

"It was our banker that told us about Darrel's accident this week. I had to call around to get the details and how to get here. It's really sad. Darrel had so much potential putting together big deals and for making money. Matter of fact, my husband's investment advisor encouraged us to buy stock in Methane Red Gas & Energy, which is owned by Mrs. Emerson," as she revealed her connection to the Emerson's.

I quickly responded, "Tyler, I'll make sure you meet Mrs. Sara Emerson after the burial. The Alter and Rosary Society, the women of the church, will be serving a light lunch right after the interment. You can meet Sara and Darrel's family back at the church.

A black hearse and two black limousines led the funeral procession for the short drive to the Sakatah Cemetery on Cemetery Lane.

Tyler and I were in the middle of the motorcade as it slowly wound around the cemetery grounds while many mourners were leaving their cars and walking to the gravesite. There was a black iron gateway hanging over the roadway leading into the Emerson Family Memorial Gardens at the very southern end of the Catholic burial grounds.

Tyler spoke while we were walking towards the burial site, "I remember the day when Darrel bought these three acres of land from his father. Their farm borders on the south side of the cemetery. Darrel paid his family an unreasonable amount of forty thousand dollars to have this section set aside in the Sakatah

Community Cemetery. After getting the deed from the county, he gave the land to the church, stipulating that all of the Emerson heirs were to be laid to rest in the prepaid burial grounds near their ancestors."

She concluded, "I thought it was very generous of him until I realized it was a huge tax deduction. Now he can reap the rewards of his hard work. He always wanted to be buried near his family."

The classy woman held my arm as we walked across the freshly mowed grass, carefully stepping around the hundreds of flowers that were beautifully planted throughout the memorial park. The scenic surroundings were calming to the soul.

Darrel Emerson was finally at peace.

The priest said a prayer as the relatives made 'the sign of the cross' and Sara Emerson placed a single white rose on the golden casket. The immediate families stood by as all mourners walked pass the gravesite placing red roses on Emerson's 'last ride.'

I was impressed with the show of love and devotion thinking to myself, "Here lays a man in sheep's clothing without anyone knowing he was a wolf."

"Amen."

As the priest encouraged the family to reassemble at the church for lunch, two US Marshals walked over to the mortician near the gravesite.

The government officials exposed their badges instructing Emerson's uncle to open the casket before lowering it into the

Living in a Lie

ground. "We have a Federal Court Order instructing you to unlock the casket so we can verify the body. We want to see the corpse and take pictures as evidence of Darrel Emerson's death."

Darrel Emerson's mother cried aloud, "Please let my son rest in peace. He is in God's hands not the US Government's. Go away and let us mourn our son's death. You have no right to interrupt our religious traditions."

The mortician spoke, "As the County Coroner, I have certified Darrel Emerson's death. You can obtain a copy at the funeral home."

Sara stepped back from the casket and glanced towards me. I was dumbfounded, unable to say anything, asking myself, "How would they have known about Emerson's exit plans? I'm not sure if I knew."

The County Sheriff, who went to high school with Darrel, stepped forward, "All due respect officers, is this necessary? If it is so important for the government to verify the body, why didn't you stop by the funeral home earlier? Why do this now? You are disrupting a sacred ceremony of the Catholic Church."

The US Marshal restated his directive, "By Order of the US Government, we are ordered to verify the body of Darrel James Emerson before entombment."

In all of the years as a PI, I had never witnessed such a misfortune of the law. Never has the federal government intervened minutes before the burial. I felt it was an outrage and insensitive to the bereaving family. No one could do anything to intervene. The family did not have time to call their attorney to get an injunction.

These two government thugs were going to have it their way.

Again, one officer stated, "As a Licensed Mortician and a Certified County Coroner, you must open the casket as hereby ordered. If you do not, we will have no other option but to pry the lid open to verify the body."

All of the family members shouted, "No!!" The elder Emerson, Darrel's father, stepped forward. "If you must, please give our deceased son some dignity and return his body to the funeral home and open the casket in private."

At that moment, a local County Judge stepped forward and suggested the family should leave so the funeral director could discreetly open the lid, if for only a brief moment. The Marshals could then verify the corpse, take the photographs and document Emerson's identity. At that calming moment, everyone conceded. The US Government had finally cornered the con man, Darrel Emerson, and wanted to be sure he was on his way to a judgment day greater then the US Federal Courts.

The Emerson clan walked away with bitterness as Sara waited to see the lid open up. The funeral director reached inside to unzip the burial bag. Those of us that stood nearby could see that Darrel James Emerson was inside, **dead**.

Living in a Lie

Chapter Nine

Haunting Past

SARA CRIED AS THE LID of her husband's casket closed again for the last time glancing directly at me with a slight grin.

Just as the mortician lowered the cover, I caught a glimpse of Emerson's left arm. What happened to Emerson's Gold Rolex watch? It was missing from his arm. I knew I saw it the day before. I specifically remember feeling troubled that such an expensive piece of jewelry would be buried never to be seen again.

"Hmm," I suddenly looked at Sara.

I could only guess what she was thinking, "Darrel, my loving husband. I still have friends and relatives around these parts, as you do. My brother was all to happy to accommodate your likely demise. God save his soul."

The US Marshals walked away from the gravesite shaking their heads in disbelief.

Coincidentally, Sara's brother Curt had contacted her one week earlier after his release from the Minnesota State Hospital in St Peter. In 1990, the Hennepin County Sheriff apprehended him for violating the conditions of his early parole. Hennepin County authorities received a complaint from Darrel Emerson notifying them of Curt Harrison's violation.

Curt's release was on September 5. He returned to his hometown of Waterville and began snooping around without anyone taking notice. He caught word that Darrel Emerson had returned to the rural community to visit his family and friends over the Labor Day weekend.

Monday night September 6

Curt was watching Darrel enter the only funeral home in town with his uncle. Curt wanted to know what was going on so he forced opened an obscure service door to the funeral home to eavesdrop on Darrel and his uncle. The cunning men were discussing a plot on how to get Darrel out of the country after his fake death on Tuesday. Darrel's uncle would hide Emerson away in a basement apartment under the funeral home until after the Friday viewing.

Living in a Lie

Before the five o'clock viewing for the immediate family, the mortician would inject a strong sedative to keep Emerson's body from moving while lying in the coffin. The two men contemplated how to remove Darrel's motionless body from the casket afterwards. Later that night, his uncle would get Darrel out of the building and secretly transport him to Shager Park where an accomplice would be waiting in an Econo Van.

Before the two men were to leave the area, Darrel's uncle would retrieve the hidden stash of money from under the rocks and give the briefcase to the driver.

Upon hearing the clever conspiracy, Curt called his sister, Sara, to get instructions on what he should do. The news did not surprise her. Instead, she was motivated to disrupt her husband's escape.

"Curt, this is what I want you to do," as she guided her mentally unstable brother on how to intervene in the consummation.

"Friday evening, when the mortician leaves the funeral home for dinner with the family, I want you to enter the morgue and place a plastic bag over Emerson's head until he quits breathing. Leave the bag in place for the mortician to find," Sara guided Curt.

"Get out of town immediately and drive up to Shager Park to retrieve the briefcase. I expect there will be money inside. Take the money and leave the state. Do not contact anyone or me until

Thanksgiving weekend," the conniving diva ordered her demented brother.

What a grand plan. What could the mortician do when he returns to find Darrel's dead body? He cannot tell the sheriff of Darrel's deceptive plans to leave the country. That would implicate him in a conspiracy, creating a fraud, aiding and abetting a fugitive from prosecution; conspiracy to defraud the IRS and the US Government.

If by chance Curt were to be arrested for suffocating Emerson, what would be the charge? Murdering a corpse? Sick!!! Not likely.

When the coroner returned and found Emerson dead in the casket, he spent the night preparing the corpse for the prearranged phony funeral without anyone knowing about the murder.

Sara, had an alibi... she was with me.

No one would suspect Curt. Only Sara knew of his whereabouts. She used her brother's contempt for her husband to kill the same man who was planning to leave her in order to avoid prosecution.

They got away with murder and Emerson got what he deserved. He was the only victim of his final scam.

When Sara Harrison-Blake-Emerson left the gravesite that September day her last words were, "My life was not a lie... you were. You used me and then deserted me. I hope God will have mercy on your soul."

"AMEN."

Chapter Ten

Widow's Defense

MONDAY MORNING, SARA WOKE TO chaos in front of her Wayzata mansion. As she looked out the second floor window, she saw two black sedans parked in the driveway and five government agents wearing FBI jackets talking to her oldest son. Without a doubt, the United States Government had started its persecution of Emerson's legacy by serving Mrs. Emerson a court order for Search and Seizure. The fight for assets and property rights had started.

Her husband's creditors had filed a class action suit to reclaim their losses, while the IRS had claims for back taxes and unpaid taxes. SEC had charges pending for security fraud, mail fraud, investment fraud, illegal stock registration and larceny.

A Federal Circuit Court had issued search warrants and ordered the FBI to begin the seizure of property and start foreclosure procedures to take possession of all the Emersons' assets. Their bank accounts were seized while the local Sheriff impounded the family's vehicles.

Lacking any notice or legal representation, Sara and her family would immediately become homeless, penniless and treated like convicted criminals. All she could do was call me for help.

I arrived within an hour to see Sara, her five kids and her mother sitting in the kitchen watching the government agents hurling their personal items into black garbage bags. Without any concern for damaging the furniture, the army of official thugs destroyed everything throughout the expensive home.

While acting like an attorney, I informed the supervising officer, "Mrs. Emerson and her family have legal rights to their personal property. You are violating their Rights to Privacy, right to council and her rights to obtain a Writ of Prohibition. You are to "cease and desist" until a court gives you specific orders to confiscate marital property or the property of innocent bystanders."

The agents immediately stopped as the senior officer spoke, "And who might you be?"

"I'm Redmond Herring, Esquire. I speak on behalf of Sara Emerson, her mother and her children. Mrs. Emerson has a right to a Widow's Right of Election until the Courts can decide otherwise. Unless you have specific orders stating the names of these innocent bystanders, you are violating their Rights

Living in a Lie

to Privacy. Your orders do not make it clear the names of any individuals living or visiting these premises."

"Please cease and desist and leave until you have the authority to confiscate the personal property of these innocent bystanders."

The officer stops but threatened to return with a court order naming all the inhabitants.

"All rise Hear ye. Hear ye. The Honorable Fourth District Court Judge Andrew Montgomery will preside in these matters," the Clerk of Court forcefully bellows out his declaration as everyone stands.

A tall stocky black man enters the courtroom from behind the bench, looks at the litigants while sitting in a high back leather chair and begins reviewing the stack of legal documents. He addresses the clerk, "Are all parties present?"

"Yes, your honor," the stern looking silver-haired clerk replies while standing before the judge.

"The matters of the United States Internal Revenue Services, US Securities and Exchange Commission, US Attorney General and the US Postal Services; also to include the State of Minnesota Department of Revenue, Minnesota Attorney General, the Shareholders of Red Rover Project, Redstone Investments, Red Earth Properties,

Redwood Industries, Methane Red Gas & Energy, Red River Developments...

...versus

The Estate of Darrel James Emerson; his widow, Sara Lorraine Blake-Emerson; Emerson Holdings, LLC; and Susan Emerson, CEO, the only stockholder of the Red Energy Development Industries of Las Vegas, Nevada," the clerk recites to the court for all the litigants to hear.

"Are all parties represented by counsel?" The powerful judge inquires.

The courtroom erupts with a solemn but forceful response, "Yes, your honor."

"Will the US Attorney please stand and review the complaints and charges against the defendants?" the judge takes control of the assembly.

"Your honor, local State and County Authorities including the US Marshal and the FBI, have orders to confiscate the assets of the deceased Darrel James Emerson's estate; his widow, Sara Emerson's joint marital and business assets; the assets of his daughter, Susan Emerson. In addition, the bank accounts and assets of Emerson Holdings need to be held in escrow and managed by a Court appointed executor until all parties, noted herein, can settle their financial claims and the lawsuits against the Emerson estate and the family's assets," the US Attorney narrates the petitioners' assertions for the judge to consider.

Judge Montgomery then looked at the respondents to ask, "Is there one attorney that can respond for all parties?"

"No, your Honor. Each party has a separate and distinctive rebuttal. Mr. Emerson's Estate has been sued by a Certified Class Action of Investors; the widow of the deceased; Shareholders of Emerson Holdings; the daughter of the deceased, Susan Emerson. The US Government and the State of Minnesota are overreaching in their respective authority violating the Constitutional Rights of innocent parties, violating the Right to Due Process, as well as denying Mrs. Emerson's Right of Election and Writ of Prohibition," the senior looking lawyer, Benjamin Levi, explains to the Court.

Attorney Raymond Thompson stands to speak before the legal assembly, "Your Honor, if I might speak?"

He gets a nod from the judge.

"Your Honor, Mr. Darrel Emerson was laid to rest just a week ago and these government lawyers want to seize personal and marital assets without any consideration for my client, Sara Emerson's responsive arguments and claims. The government's actions are without due process and unconstitutional. Mrs. Emerson and Mr. Emerson's heirs have a right to present their claims in a court of law before subordinate parties sequester or seize any jointly owned assets," Attorney Thompson states before the Judge.

"Your Honor, may I address the Court?" Attorney Ronald Lee stands.

Judge Montgomery responds but seems agitated with the third attorney standing in front of his bench, "Yes. Who is your client? What do you have to say?"

"Thank you your honor. I represent Mr. Emerson's Estate and Emerson Holdings, a Limited Liability Corporation, registered and located in West Palm Beach, Florida. The government wants to foreclose and seize assets by an Ex Parte Injunction without proper notice to adverse parties. The respondents, including my client, were not served notice nor were they granted application for contesting the government claims. The petitioners along with the government have held a Kangaroo Court without legal authority, disregarding the rights afforded to all citizens of this country. All Orders for Seizure and Foreclosure are fraudulent and are not legally binding."

The judge responds cautiously, "Do the government and noted petitioners have a rebuttal?"

"Yes, your honor," US Attorney, Charles Carver stands to address the court.

"Mr. Emerson was given ample notice to these matters that have been pending for over six months. Upon learning of Mr. Emerson's death, US Federal Magistrate Thomas Zachary ordered all assets of Darrel Emerson be seized and held in escrow until all pending litigation can be resolved."

"I can assure this court that Magistrate Zachary will not appreciate his court being portrayed as a Kangaroo Court. Mr. Emerson was well aware of these matters. If he had not died, the US Marshals were ready to arrest him as a flight risk, until all pending litigation could be concluded," the US Attorney responds with self-confidence that his assertions would triumph all other arguments in the courtroom.

Attorney Ronald Lee stands and objects to the US Attorney's summary, "Your Honor, until an Evidentiary Hearing is held in all these matters, the government cannot take private property and personal assets from US Citizens without due process. A fair and reasonable trial before a US District Court Judge or a Federal Circuit Judge must hear all the findings of facts before recommending disposition and a subsequent order. Without a Certified Court Order, no Action for Foreclosure can be executed."

Attorney Raymond Thompson stands to make his motion, "Your Honor, the Respondents in these matters hereby motion the Court to Limit Sequestration, Foreclosure and Confiscation of anyone's assets until such Notice is ordered by an authorized District Court Judge as a Matter of Law."

Judge Montgomery taps his gavel to demand order before summarizing his opinion, "After hearing from opposing council in these matters, this Court hereby Orders all Seizure Actions to Cease until further notice. In addition, I hereby order all parties to begin litigation to resolve all complaints within appropriate District Court Jurisdictions."

The judge bangs his gavel one more time, "This hearing is hereby closed until further notice. You are all dismissed." He steps down, takes leave of the bench, and enters his private chambers.

All the lawyers pack up their papers and begin to leave the courtroom as Sara Emerson and Susan Emerson hug each other before exiting with their respective attorneys. I sat in the back of the room watching the proceedings with Tyler Castor.

As the Emerson women walk towards the rear of the courtroom, I motioned for Sara to step near me to hear my suggestion. "Sara, let's walk over to Murray's for lunch and discuss this mess that Darrel created. God rest his soul. We need to evaluate all your options. Tyler, can you join us? Your insights into Darrel's financial dealings might help Sara get through these matters."

It did not take long before Sara broke down and began crying as we all settled into the booth for lunch, hoping to find some solitude to the nightmare Darrel Emerson bestowed on his favorite women. The only thing that was accomplished in the US Federal Court was delaying the inevitable. Sara and her stepdaughter would soon be penniless and impoverished by the government and hundreds of disgruntled investors would bankrupt them. Darrel knew his investment schemes were unraveling and collapsing after years of avoidance and deceit.

Living in a Lie

I sat calmly listening to the women share their repugnance for the charmed executive they once loved. I wondered who was at fault for not questioning Emerson's undeserving wealth and prosperity. He had not been open and honest while secretly leading them down a path of irresistible luxury as his house of fraud made them victims of their own greed.

We all knew this day would come. The deep well of indiscretion finally caught up to this con artist, as the endless spigot of money dried up. The illusionary bubble had burst.

How would Sara Blake-Emerson survive another disappointing marriage that would leave her without the wealth she always wanted?

I finally broke the silence of self-pity by introducing my insights to the legal process that was about to impugn their dignity by saying, "I have a radical idea to reduce your impending legal costs and forego your public embarrassment. You will not have to answer for Darrel's encumbrances."

With that profound statement, the two beautiful women stopped eating and focused on my looming words of wisdom.

"Sara, have a lawyer file for a divorce."

Tyler responded, "Redmond, are you out of your mind? Darrel is deceased. What difference would it make? When a husband dies, his widow gets everything."

I responded with a smug look, "Exactly, including all the debts. If she were to petition the Catholic Church for an annulment and then petition the District Family Court, she could divorce Darrel's debts which are greater then his assets."

"Subsequently, any jointly held marital assets would be subjected to only fifty percent sequestration. As I understand, Darrel Emerson did not have any interests or ownership in the investment firm in South Dakota. So therefore, the Courts cannot attach or sequester Sara's personal assets or her solely owned business assets. In addition, the five hundred thousand dollar life insurance policy will help you pay your legal bills while the government tries to foreclose on your assets. Meanwhile, I suggest you buy a modest house for your family and downsize your automobiles. Maybe Tyler and her husband can get you a good deal on some newer/used cars."

Sara responded to my proposal, "Redmond, your suggestions make more sense then spending the next two years fighting with the government trying to keep that which is not mine."

Living in a Lie

Chapter Eleven

Don't Ask

THE WARM FALL WEATHER OF September had cooled as the northern winds of October blew across Minnesota and a flurry of legal motions, affidavits and supporting evidence bristled between council. Attorneys in Florida served papers on attorneys in Nevada. Federal lawyers served notices to attorneys in South Dakota and in Minnesota.

Sara quietly hired a private attorney to expedite her divorce and annulment in order to avoid any possible prosecution even after he advised her of her rights. "Spouses do not have to testify in any court ordered discovery after the death of a loved one."

By mid-October, the United States Attorney General had intimidated Emerson's daughter, Susan, to plea bargain and give testimony to aid the Federal Government. She agreed to cooperate by documenting her father's fraudulent business activities, his pyramid schemes and his secret bank accounts.

Darrel Emerson's financial empire was falling apart as investors and creditors testified before a Federal Judge in Minneapolis. All petitioners and aggrieved parties wanted restitution forcing the Court Appointed Executor to bankrupt the estate.

When Sara learned of her stepdaughter's avoidance, she called her, "Why are you forsaking your father and helping the government? Nothing will be granted to Darrel's heirs or to me."

Susan rejected Sara's plea, "Why should I be held accountable for my father's lies and his dishonest business dealings? I did nothing wrong. He cheated me out of my inheritance and deceived hundreds of people out of their life savings."

Sara began to cry, "Honey, if you testify for the government, you'll be against me. I'll lose everything including the house on Lake Minnetonka, my Jaguar and the condo in Cabos San Lucas. They are trying to confiscate everything, even my jewelry."

The widow purposely concealed any knowledge of the investment firm in South Dakota and the recent sale of the cabin in northern Minnesota, mostly because she could no longer trust her stepdaughter. If Susan was going to help the executor of Emerson's Estate, Sara must hide any undisclosed assets. However, her real concerns were the US Marshals discovering how Emerson died in his coffin the night before his funeral.

Susan's next query caused anxiety for Sara, "Sara, do you know what happened to my father's Rolex watch? I'm sure I saw it on his arm in his casket during the viewing. I called my great uncle, the mortician, and he told me it was <u>not</u> on my father's body when the Marshals ordered the coffin opened at the gravesite."

I received Sara's call the night before the next discovery hearing was scheduled to be in front of a Federal Judge. "Red, I need to talk to you tonight. I'm worried about Susan's testimony. Can I come over for the night? I'll pack a bag."

I had no idea if the Feds had tapped my phone but I was certain they were tracking all of Sara's calls. I did not know if they knew where I lived so I replied with caution, "Sara, meet me at Davanni's. How soon can you be there?" responding to her plea.

"Possibly, in an hour," she replied. "After we eat, can we light up your fireplace? I'll bring some wine."

Well, if the Feds were listening they now knew that Sara and I were lovers. That private information might initiate an investigation into our longstanding relationship. I could be indicted for various indiscretions while working for Sara and when I had worked for her deceased husband.

I knew I had to be careful and questioned Sara's motives. Could she be helping the Feds uncover my crimes in order get leniency for her misdeeds?

I had always been wary not to disclose my surreptitious operations to anyone, especially to Sara. However, she might speculate my involvement in her current affairs was not a coincidence. Did Emerson divulge my assignments to her to ease his own conscience?

It was six o'clock when Sara parked her silver Jaguar near the front door of the restaurant. I looked vigilantly for any signs of the Feds or any undercover surveillance agents. Thankfully, she was not being followed by anyone.

As Sara walked into the building, I was surprised to see her in causal clothes wearing a baseball cap, sneakers, tight blue jeans and a brown leather flight jacket.

After writing a message on a napkin, "Be careful for what you say... they could be listening," I handed it to her as she greeted me. Then I asked her for her cell phone and took the batteries out to avoid being tracked by any government agents.

Sara spoke first, "Red, can I talk openly now?"

"Yes, I think its safe. What's going on with Susan?"

"She has become a witness for the prosecutor. I'm concerned she might raise questions about Darrel's death and the circumstances surrounding his funeral. When I spoke to her, she asked about her father's Rolex watch. She even called the mortician in Waterville questioning him."

I responded, "She could become a real problem if she convinces the Feds to investigate Darrel's death. Sara, what happened to the watch?"

"Red, why do you ask me?" Sara responded with an angry attitude.

I explained, "Sara, both Tyler and I noticed the watch was missing when the US Marshal demanded the casket be opened before the mortician lowered Darrel's body into his grave. The watch was on his arm the day before at the review. Do you think Darrel's uncle took the watch before sealing the casket? I think there are laws against stealing from a corpse."

"I don't know. Nevertheless, Susan has become a liability and could disrupt my business in South Dakota. If the Feds interrogate her, they might find out things that could hurt both of us," Sara concluded.

"Sara, are you suggesting that I intervene and cause her to disappear? If I were to do something, the Feds would certainly start an investigation. Now is not the time to tamper with their witness," I tried to explain.

"Red, I fear her testimony could uncover many wrongful deeds which would cause the Feds to start countless investigations as well. If she were missing, that is all they will have; 'A Missing Witness.' She is the government's only source to our past. No one else will cooperate and incriminate themselves," the nervous woman quietly stated.

"Sara, can you get your attorney to cause a delay in tomorrow's hearing?" I inquired.

"What can I suggest to him?" she responded.

"Have your lawyer move for an Extension of Discovery because you (the widow) have found undisclosed assets that need to be documented before the Court and before any government witness should testify. He should advise the court that you will disclose all known assets in order to avoid perjuring yourself. You have a right to correct the record to the best of your ability."

"The Judge must allow new findings to be entered and documented before the prosecution can charge you or anyone else with perjury. Have your lawyer challenge the prosecutor 'not to charge anyone (particularly you) with perjury' if the court finds evidence contrary to your testimony. Neither the Judge nor the prosecutor will agree to that challenge because the government is trying to circumvent your status as widow. They want to charge you with perjury in order to take precedence over your Right of Election, otherwise known as a Widow's Election."

I continued explaining my strategy to her, "The Judge must allow you to enter more findings by affidavits and supporting documentation. Your attorney should ask for a continuance for at least ten days to allow you to document your findings. This will delay the executor's testimony and the government's counter witness testimony. That will give me time to purge their witness."

"But, Red," Sara interrupted, "What assets will I disclose to the court that the government does not know about?"

"Sara, the government is trying to sequester the big ticket items that Darrel purchased through his holding company in Florida, such as your home and condo, your yacht and other boats, your automobiles and any expensive jewelry that he owned. They already know about his Red Energy Development Industries in Las Vegas that took money from your business in Sioux Falls.

His daughter Susan was the CEO. Here's what you instruct your lawyer to do... at the next hearing he should submit your Divorce Decree, your Annulment Decree from the church, a notice of a lawsuit against Susan Emerson and Red Energy Development Industries for fraud, embezzlement and unauthorized transfer of money from your South Dakota Investment Firm."

"In addition, have your attorney submit a motion proclaiming your immunity from testifying under the Marital Communication Doctrine which exempts you for the one year you were married to Darrel. Then have your lawyer submit your affidavit declaring the listing of joint marital property cannot be sequestered until the Divorce Court submits its findings and orders a Division of Marital Assets. Have your attorney submit a copy of your Corporate Bylaws, Certificates of Stock Ownership and an affidavit proclaiming you, as the CEO, President and Sole Stockholder, stating that Darrel Emerson had no authority in your investment firm."

"Your business assets cannot be seized by the government, the IRS nor any of Darrel's past creditors without cause," I concluded my legal advice.

"Wow. So therefore, my assets and personal property along with my family's personal property are exempt from the government's claims until proven otherwise. Is that what I can expect?" Sara concluded her understanding of all the legal maneuvers that I had just recited.

"You got it, pretty lady. Darrel told me that you would be able to defend yourself and survive the government's attacks." At that point, I quickly realized I mistakenly disclosed a confidential connection to her husband's intentions. Damn it.

"Sara lets go to my place and have some wine in front of a warm fire. Follow me and be sure to park your car in my garage," I wanted to move things along before she had time to question my 'slip of the tongue.' I paid the bill before we drove away heading towards an amorous night of sexual pleasure.

———————

Chapter Twelve

Brotherly Love

It WAS THREE O'CLOCK IN the morning on Friday, the day after Thanksgiving, when the telephone began ringing as it sat on the nightstand next to Sara's queen size bed. She awoke with a bad attitude towards the insensitive caller as she rolled over to reach the irritating device.

"Hello, who is this rude caller?" she asserted her anger. "I was sound asleep and you have upset me."

"Sara, it's Curt," a soft spoken voice whispered in her ear.

"Curt, do not say a thing. Can you meet me today?" Sara immediately sat up in bed and was now completely awake.

"Yes," the voice responded. "Where?"

"Let me think a minute... can you meet me at your favorite A&W Restaurant south of the Twin Cities? I can be there by noon. Will that work for you?"

"Yes, I'll be there," the secretive caller hung up.

Sara pulled the bedclothes over her head as her mind swirled with dozens of questions. She could not sleep and was anxious with worry for the meeting she had just scheduled with her brother. He did as she had advised him to do in September and now had returned needing more direction from his intuitive sister.

Curt was not a perceptive person, he was quite naive, careless with an angry attitude for most of his life. Oftentimes, his eyes would glaze over in a conversation and he was easily distracted losing continuity in his purpose. Sara and her six other siblings concluded that their youngest brother had hypertension dysfunctional disorder since he was eight or nine years old.

As she curled up under the down comforter, her thoughts began to recollect the Harrison's family history beginning in the 1960's when they lived in Waterville, Minnesota. Something or some event changed Curt's passive personality. His anger would often explode and scare the entire family until their father would beat Curt into submission with a belt. The Christian household was always edgy with concerns that the 'devil had the boy's soul.'

Living in a Lie

Friends in the local Baptist Church would pray openly for the Harrison family's safety. Everyone in town knew of Curt's mental problems but no one knew how to silence his demons.

The family dynamics changed in 1967 when Curt carelessly pointed a shotgun at his older sister, Carla, accidentally shooting her in the chest, killing her immediately. Curt was trying to prevent his sister from telling their father about the younger boy's inappropriate sexual contact. Only Curt knew the complete story. Everyone, including the County Sheriff, considered the death an accident.

Thirty years ago, there were no family counselors or psychologists to help Curt through his anger problems. The family prayed together often hoping that God would hear their plea and rid the boy of his evil spirits.

Sara in her grief and sadness moved out of state to finish her last year in high school, away from the memories of her beloved sister's death. She hated her brother and was relieved when he left home and went to work as an over-the-road truck driver.

Curt had many problems over the past twenty years including incarceration for murdering two young female hitchhikers. After he received a parole from a ten year prison sentence, the state sent him to the St Peter Hospital for his psychological problems.

So much had happened in the past three months since her husband's death and funeral in Waterville.

Her last conversation with her brother was cloudy with all the other events. She did remember advising him to leave the state without contacting any other family members and to stay away until this holiday. Now that he was back, she needed to be cautious and secretive not to alert anyone, especially the government.

"Curt, I'm happy to see you. How have you been?" Sara greets her younger brother. "We need to sit in your truck in case the FBI might have wired my car. Things have been crazy for me since Darrel's death. It's hard to know who I can trust."

"I'm ok. I'm living in Indiana. I was able to buy a house and some property near Louisville. No one knows anything of my past. I like to be alone," the thirty-year-old skinny man replied as they walked out of the A&W in Faribault.

Curt unlocked the passenger door for Sara and made small talk until he could settle in behind the steering wheel.

Sara was anxious to question her estranged brother about his presence in Waterville on Labor Day weekend, "Curt, after you left the funeral home did anyone see you or follow you out of town?"

"I don't think so. I did find the briefcase that Darrel mentioned to his uncle. In it was two hundred and fifty, hundred dollar bills and this envelope inside. I did not open it. But I'm curious to know what is in it," the truck driver responded as he handed the white letter size envelope to his sister.

As she began opening the envelope, she instructed him, "Do not say anything to our family or anyone else about this. So far, no one has questioned the circumstances surrounding Darrel's

Living in a Lie

death. Not even his uncle. You must live your life away from here without contacting anyone for at least five years. Keep the money but do not spend it carelessly. The government is trying to find all of Darrel's money. It is best you just stay away and stay out of trouble. Do not call or contact anyone in Minnesota."

"What's in the envelope, Sara?" Curt questions her.

"It looks like a coded message to me. I'll have to have someone else decipher the words," she responded.

"Curt, you must leave the state and return to your home; today," she directs him. "Thank you for meeting me."

Sara gives her brother a hug, steps out of the man's truck and walks over to her Jaguar, looking for any undercover agents that might be listening or watching.

The Harrison siblings drove away from the rendezvous without looking back each heading in a different direction.

Chapter Thirteen

Greed Can't Wait

IT WAS HARD FOR SARA to restrain herself from calling but she knew the Feds could be tapping her phone and tracking her car. She exited off 35W at Old Shakopee Road in Bloomington and then drove to Byerlys to call to me.

"Redmond, I need to see you as soon as possible. I'm in East Bloomington and can be at your town house in fifteen minutes. Will that be ok?" her familiar voice requested my cooperation.

"Sure, pull your car in the garage. I'll be looking for you," I replied with trepidation not knowing if the Feds were listening to my phone calls or watching my home.

It was almost three o'clock when Sara pulled into my garage, turned off the engine and got out of her Jaguar while the garage door closed to the floor. We hugged and entered the house.

Living in a Lie

November is usually cold in Minnesota. The temperature was hovering around thirty degrees with a few snow flurries blowing through the brown lawns.

Sara kept her pure white wool sweater on while I heated up some coffee in the kitchen. I could tell she was nervous and uneasy as we sat near the wood burning fireplace.

"What is going on Sara? Where have you been?" I asked her with concern.

"Redmond, early this morning my brother called and I agreed to meet him in Faribault. I'm returning from that meeting with this mysterious envelope that Curt found in a briefcase Darrel hid near Cannon Lake. Curt is keeping the cash that he found in the case. This envelope is obviously from Darrel," she handed the papers over to me.

The sheet of paper inside the envelope was not for anyone nor was it like a normal letter. There was a long paragraph of maybe one hundred words typed continuously without any punctuation or logical sentences. It was a random grouping of letters with random spacing. It made no sense and had no pattern. I conclude it was a code of some sort to disguise a message.

"How much money was in the briefcase?" I questioned her.

"Curt said there was only twenty-five thousand dollars. He used the money for a down payment on a house in Indiana," she replied.

"Sara, I'll need some time to decipher this. Give me a couple of days and I'll get back to you. Are you planning to spend the evening with me?" I inquired hoping her answer would be yes.

Over the past three years, she was always responsive when I initiated sexual contact. On that cold November evening, I had a lot to be thankful for.

Nine-thirty AM...

"Redmond, it was a delightful evening, I need to be going. Thanks for breakfast, It is almost ten and I have a phone conference at eleven with people in South Dakota. I'm trying to sell the Red Methane Gas Converter to the inventor and new group of investors," the sophisticated woman explained.

"I understand. I'll call you when I solve Darrel's puzzle. Good luck with the Feds," I helped her with her coat as she prepared to leave my home.

I was anxious to look at Emerson's secret message. (I wondered if he had documented the locations of the eight cases of money transported from the Cayman Islands three months ago.) It only made sense that he would keep the destinations concealed by code until he or someone else needed to retrieve the cache.

The only clues I knew of were 8 private couriers flying from the island to 8 different destinations, on 8 different private jets,

Living in a Lie

on the 6th day of the 9th month of 1993. I did not know the dates of Emerson's birth so I considered calling Sara but hesitated knowing the Feds might be listening. Then I remembered I had a copy of Darrel's obituary. November 22, 1945. (11, 22, 1945).

By adding up all the numbers except the year numbers, the total was 72. I divided 72 by 8, which equals 9. Emerson started with 9 accounts. His funeral was on September 11, 1993. There are nine-9s and there are eight-8s. I had no idea which number I should use... nines or eights. I tried using the number 9 to crack the code; that did not work nor did the number 8.

———————

"Sara, this is Red. We need to meet soon. Call me," was the message I left on her voice recorder.

Within the hour she called back, "Red, I can you meet on Wednesday at our favorite restaurant. How about lunch?"

We agreed.

———————

As always, I arrived fifteen minutes early to check out the parking lot and the patrons inside the restaurant. There were no suspicious activities in the area so I relaxed with a cup of French Vanilla coffee and began reading the morning Star & Tribune. A headline for an article in the business section left me speechless.

"Minnetonka Woman Loses South Dakota Business as Federal Marshals raid her Investment Firm."

The article recited all the events leading up to the sequestration by the FBI, SEC and the IRS. The investment firm was Methane Red Gas & Energy, LLC.

Wow!!! Will Sara survive another setback? I did not expect the government would move so fast. The article disclosed the government's extensive investigation that started six months ago while they were tracking Darrel Emerson. His schemes brought them to the widow's doorstep.

I had to assume our lunch date would be canceled not knowing if Sara would show up now that her entire financial world had been seized. I decided to wait a little longer. I could not call any of her phone numbers. I waited fifteen minutes hoping my portable phone would ring. It did not.

There was no sign of her in the parking lot as I waited for her call. After another thirty minutes, I drove home.

There were no messages on my home phone message recorder and I knew I could not call any of her numbers. I would have to wait until she contacted me.

Maybe Darrel Emerson had miscalculated his wife's resolve to fend off the Feds? Was she in custody or at a relative's home or hiding in her mansion on Lake Minnetonka? I had no way of knowing.

After eating a sandwich and some tomato soup, I laid down on the couch in front of a burning fire. My mind was rushing through dozens of scenarios that might explain Sara's absence. What is happening? What happened to all that money that I know was in the briefcase?

When the fire burned out, a cold chill hovered throughout my darkened living room. A winter storm was blowing in from the Southwest bringing freezing temperatures and a couple of inches of snow.

It was Thursday morning, December 2, 1993 and I had slept through the night.

No one called. There were no messages on the recording machine. No one had knocked on the door nor were there any tire tracks in the snow. Everything was dead silent.

I turned on the radio to WCCO Morning News to hear the reports of school closings and the weather statistics. Throughout the night, the Twin Cities had received nearly ten inches of snow. Travel was difficult and many businesses closed.

Here I was in the middle of the wintry tundra without much food, running low on wine and no one to keep me warm.

Where in the world is Sara?

I made a couple of frustrating calls to Sara's lawyers without any results. The snow and cold forced many people to stay home for the day. After leaving a number of messages, Attorney Ronald Lee finally returned my call. "Mr. Herring, how can I help you?"

"I'm trying to contact Sara Emerson. After reading the article in the newspaper about the government's seizure of her business in South Dakota, I need to offer her my support and assistance," I quickly responded to his inquiry.

"Mr. Herring, I have not heard from her. All of her utilities have been disconnected. I can only assume that she is without financial resources to pay her bills. Until I hear from her, my firm will suspend our representation. I did get notice from the US Attorney that the Court has ordered all her assets to be sequestered until the Court Appointed Trustee sorts out the Emerson Estate," the notable counselor informed me.

"If by chance you hear from her, please tell her that I need to talk with her," those were my last words as I hung up. I had received more information from her attorney than expected.

Now I was concerned for Sara's safety. I knew she would not contact Darrel Emerson's daughter, Susan, since their disagreement.

I knew her first husband would not help her. They were still fighting in court over child support and marital assets, after three years.

Sara had mentioned an attorney in Sioux Falls who wanted her investment firm as a client. After making a few calls, I finally found the sole practitioner, Thomas Allen.

Living in a Lie

I presented a brief introduction and then began my inquiry, "Mr. Allen, Sara Emerson has disappeared since the government seized her assets and took control of her manufacturing plant in Brookings. Can you shed some light on all of this? What have you heard?"

"Well, Mr. Herring, I can only tell you what I'm hearing from the locals some of which might be rumor. This past Wednesday the Feds raided her firm, confiscated all documents and records in Methane Red Gas & Energy and sequestered Mrs. Emerson's bank accounts. Word has it that US Marshals raided the manufacturing plant in Brookings sending all employees away. Our State Attorney tried to stop their activities with a Cease and Desist Order but a Magistrate in Washington, DC overruled it. Rumor has it the US Government seized the prototype Professor Daniel Alberding had moved from UND to the plant in Brookings. The FBI posted notices at the manufacturing facility stating the seizure was a 'Matter of National Security.' The government confiscated the prototype, patents and all of the engineering blueprints and locked the invention away in Washington for security reasons. The FBI arrested the professor who is being held in a Federal facility until a United States Federal Judge orders his release."

Attorney Allen continued disclosing his information, "The entire legal community throughout the state is in shock by the lawless activities. Our State Senators are traveling to DC to appeal the entire sequestration. There were no hearings in our State Courts, no local law enforcement officials were involved and the Governor's office was uninformed of the FBI's actions. It does not surprise me that Mrs. Emerson is missing. I'm guessing the US Marshals have arrested her. But let me remind you... most of what I hear is without any supporting facts."

I thanked the lawyer and hung up the phone.

What was going on? How in the world did a methane gas converter cause such security concerns? Did Darrel Emerson have a viable invention that foreign governments wanted? If so, it was worth millions, maybe billions of dollars, worldwide. Did our government seize the technology to prevent other countries from developing this revolutionary converter of clean energy?

How ironic Emerson's last investment scheme was a viable invention that would have made him an honest millionaire. He was a man of habit always working on false pretenses trying to swindle money from others never expecting his next venture would have any value.

If he had been an honest man, not stealing from his investors, the Feds and the Court may not have known of his global enterprise and seized his greatest venture.

God rest his soul.

"Sir, how can I help you?" the woman behind the mahogany desk asked as I entered the lobby of Emerson's Funeral Home in Waterville, MN.

"Yes, I'm hoping to speak to the funeral director. I believe he is also the County Coroner. I'm a private investigator from the Twin Cities looking for some information. Is Mr. Emerson available or do I need an appointment?" I responded cautiously not to alarm the small town secretary.

"You should have called before driving down here. I could have saved you the trip. Mr. Emerson is in Florida for a well needed vacation. He flew to Miami last Saturday and will return just before our busy holiday season. I expect him on the tenth. Who shall I say stopped in?" The middle-aged, overweight woman replied as she escorted me out the doors of the main lobby.

"Ms., please give him my business card and I'll call him on the twelfth. Would you have one of Mr. Emerson's business cards?" I replied as she immediately handed me the director's card.

The time had come; I needed to find the missing pieces in order to solve the puzzles that Darrel Emerson left behind. I assumed I was the only person with any knowledge of Darrel's multi-million dollar cache in the Cayman Islands. However, I had no idea who knew about the million dollars in the briefcase that I buried at Shaker Park near Cannon Lake.

As a private investigator, my instincts and my years of experience helped me to uncover the missing clues that could lead to Emerson's millions.

I called the LeSueur County Records and Deeds office inquiring to the ownership of the funeral home in Waterville, the Emerson farmstead and the shareholders of the local bank. To my surprise, a private holding corporation registered in Faribault, MN, owned all three properties. I decided to stop at the Rice County Court House and sort through their records to find the names of stockholders and any lien holders.

Faribault was a thriving community of about twenty thousand residents with many prosperous businesses and large manufacturing companies. It was the county seat located fifty miles south of the Twin Cities. In the nineteen eighties, the State built a minimum security prison for white-collar criminals after closing and razing an old state mental institution, a school for the blind and the school for the hearing impaired.

A number of major banks from the Twin Cities opened branch offices to attract local business payrolls, new home mortgages and new car loans as well as farming deposits and loans. The local financial, legal and investment industries were as sophisticated as those in the big cities. The county courts and administrative offices were always busy due to the growing economy throughout the area.

Darrel Emerson would know how to avoid government detection of large amounts of money if he could disguise his deposits as corporate payroll or revenue receipts from big companies. He knew that farmers made large deposits from cattle and grain sales.

Banking transactions, buying and selling of stock, paying dividends to shareholders and private asset investments were all part of the behind the scenes banking industry where huge sums of money transferred in and out of the banks. A bank officer could cover up large deposits and Emerson could avoid detection and federal taxes.

In the early nineties, banks and counties began converting their records to digital technology, i.e. computers. Rice County was a center of thousands of financial and legal transactions so the county had to invest in the new technology in order to streamline their services. When I began my search, thankfully, the past twenty years of county business had been transcribed and available on their computers.

My inquiries revealed many independent transactions and autonomous documents that hid Emerson's secret money transfers to his family. He was laundering millions out of his "investment firms" through his families' bank, bogus companies and secret investments hidden from the SEC. However, I had an au fait viewpoint after working with Emerson for many years, which helped me to connect the covert relationships.

Darrel and his father, his two uncles and his four brothers were all stockholders. That would be eight shareholders. Eight seemed to be the connection to the hidden cache.

The name of the holding company was Red Sky Corporation with an office located on the fourth floor in the old First Bank building on Main Street in downtown Faribault,

My adrenalin spiked with anticipation knowing I was uncovering Darrel Emerson's secrets. I felt a personal camaraderie with a master of deceit. Uncovering more and more details about the Emerson dynasty, I felt the clues were leading me closer to the eight hidden bank accounts as I connected the dots and solved the puzzle of words and numbers that were secretly sent to Sara.

I returned to the Twin Cities late in the day anxious to solve the clues to find the millions of dollars hidden throughout the world.

Chapter Fourteen

Fishing

IT WAS NOT LONG BEFORE the Emerson clan learned of my inquiries in Southern Minnesota. I could only imagine they would jump to many ill conceived conclusions; assume that I was involved in Darrel's murder and stealing the hidden briefcase full of money. Within two weeks of visiting Waterville and Faribault, I suspected the family started the fire that destroyed my town house in Bloomington. I'm sure they were hoping to kill me in the fire but, fortunately, I was spending time in a secret apartment hidden away in The Towers, on First Street, in the heart of downtown Minneapolis.

All my important records, documents and appointment diaries were stored in a safe in the two-bedroom condominium apartment that I had purchased in 1983, under the corporate name, Red Fox Investments, which was registered in Delaware.

The Towers were the best place in the Upper Midwest to hideaway. Many of the two hundred residents were State and Federal politicians, attorneys, judges and surreptitious mistresses. There was twenty-four hour security with actual guards on the premise seven days a week. Underground parking provided a hide away for personal vehicles. This fortress maintained an on site private restaurant and a private outdoor swimming pool. On the twenty-second floor, was an exclusive exercise facility with a spectacular skyline view.

All the residents kept to themselves and did not invite many outsiders into the building. The hush-hush community was exceptionally quiet. No one spoke in the elevators, in the halls or in the dinning room.

I anticipated complete anonymity; the highest security in the city without any invasion of my privacy or safety. Over the past ten years, I never once invited anyone to my sanctuary nor did I list my name with the property. All bills associated with the condominium were mailed directly to a PO Box Service Center in Delaware for Red Fox Investments. A confidential executor managed all my assets.

Years ago when I chose my line of work, my intuition told me to prepare a backup plan to evade desperate perpetrators. There have been many occasions to seek solitude and security in this cave dwelling.

"Seth, how was your trip to the cities over the weekend? Were you successful in your mission?" George Henry Emerson, the family patriarch and Darrel Emerson's father, questioned the youngest son in the dynasty.

"Pa, I found the PI's town home in West Bloomington. I think I missed our chance to snuff him out. He was not home when I broke into his place," Seth responded to his father. "I did not find any cash, documents or clues for locating Sara. I'll keep searching for the guy over the holiday."

"We'll try to catch him when he calls your uncle William at the funeral home in a couple of days. Hopefully, we can sucker him into a meeting and deal with him then," the old farmer suggested.

"Mr. Emerson, I was a friend and business associate of your nephew, Darrel Emerson. Darrel was a regular client for over ten years as I fulfilled various confidential business transactions for him. I was at his funeral in July and the reason I'm calling you is to wrap up some loose ends. Even though he has passed away, I feel an obligation to complete my assignment," I explained my reason for calling the mortician in Waterville.

"Mr. Herring, how can I help you? Maybe you should talk to Darrel's father, George. I was not involved in Darrel's business nor did I keep up on his life," William Emerson responded with a questionable tone in his voice.

"I do not feel comfortable discussing these matters over the phone. I'll be happy to drive down to Waterville at your convenience so we can talk in private. Any evening would work for me," I made the suggestion to make him feel obligated to meet me.

"Ok but I'm not sure how I can help you," the funeral director replied. "I can meet with you on Monday evening, the twenty-second. Will that work for you?"

"I can be there at five o'clock," I suggested hoping to appease him.

"Mr. Herring, that's too early. I have work to complete for a viewing on Tuesday morning. It'll have to be later, say seven PM."

"Ok, I can work with that," I answered with caution. I really wanted to enter the mortuary earlier hoping someone might notice me.

"Mr. Herring, please enter my building by the west side door. I will turn on an outside light above the doorway; inside you will find a hall leading to my office. Please ring the door bell when you arrive and I'll buzz you in," William Emerson directed my future right of entry.

"Thank you. I'll see you then," I concluded the call with some reservation. This was not the scenario I wanted.

December 22, 1993

Living in a Lie

It was a cold day as winter temperatures hovered around ten degrees Fahrenheit. The roads and highways were clean without any snow or ice; however, the lakes and rivers were frozen.

In anticipation of the long cold drive, I prepared a winter emergency kit and stowed it in the back seat of the Jeep with an extra blanket and boots. The weather in Minnesota can be brutal when wind chill temperatures go below zero.

It was an hour drive to Faribault and another half-hour to Waterville. I wanted to be earlier for my evening appointment and survey the small town during the daylight hours so I left downtown Minneapolis at three o'clock.

I felt the cold north wind blowing through the vehicle as I drove south on Interstate 35W realizing I had no backup plans if something went wrong. In all the years as a private investigator, I always felt in control of my environment but this meeting seemed uncomfortable and ill conceived.

I drove around the small town and located the police station, a gas station, the Catholic Church that Emerson grew up in, the mortuary where I would be meeting the town's only mortician, the only bank and a farm implement store. Most of the locals stay indoors during the winter months leaving the village looking like a secluded ghost town. A few hardy souls were seated in a nearby bar watching as I stopped at the lone restaurant in town to get some soup and eat a sandwich.

The only person inside was an older woman named Marie who was the waiter and the cook. She was happy to have a customer, encouraging me to sit at a table near the front window.

"Where are you from, stranger?" she asked while pouring a cup of black coffee, assuming I drank coffee.

"Ya know, hon, this is not a good night to be traveling alone out here in the country," as she continued pushing for a conversation.

"I drove in from the Twin Cities to meet with William Emerson this evening at his funeral home. I am a writer investigating Darrel Emerson's lifetime accomplishments and his family history. Maybe you can help. How long have you been in town?" I responded hoping to get more insight to the Emerson dynasty.

Two hours later of conversing with the town's 'Chatterbox' I had more gossip then I could have gotten out of the local newspaper archives. The coffee kept me warm as darkness settled over the main street. Marie uncovered years of local folklore. The Emerson family tree had had a mysterious history for over one hundred years. Their legendary families were all prominent citizens throughout the county.

It was six fifty-five when I drove into the lot near to the west side door at the funeral home as a black sedan pulled in behind me with an intense spotlight shinning into my rearview mirror. Before

I could open my car door, a local police officer was standing near me directing me to roll down the window.

"Sir, can I help you find your way? At this hour, the funeral home is usually closed. Are you lost? I do not recognize your vehicle. How can I help you?" the intimidating police officer questioned my presence.

Just as I was about to respond, William Emerson stepped out from his building and shouted at the officer, "Arty, that guy is here to see me. He has an appointment at seven PM. It's ok. Thanks for stopping to check him out. Mr. Herring, come on in."

I felt relieved and safer knowing the local police knew I was in town and meeting with the funeral director. I was concerned that no one would know if I went missing. If by chance a body would be found, in the spring, frozen solid in the ice of Sakatah Lake, at least the local police would have record of me and my Jeep parked in the Emerson Funeral Home lot, on December 22.

I gathered up my briefcase, put on my heavy parka and entered the mortuary feeling a little safer as a fresh snow covered the parking lot. I was hoping the Chief of Police would park nearby and watch the building for a while.

Mr. Emerson directed me down a flight of stairs into the basement level where he usually embalmed the deceased. All the cupboards, tabletops, moveable carts and cold storage doors were made of shining silver stainless steel. Bright white ceramic tile covered the floor.

A glass enclosed cabinet displayed an assortment of knives and other devices that made the mortician's job easier while performing his craft. I stood in front of the locked cabinet trying to position myself on 'high-ground' thinking I needed to be prepared for whatever might happen.

"Well, Mr. Herring, how can I help you?" the six-foot man stood in the shadows across the room with his arms folded in front of him.

"Mr. Emerson, I was a private confidant for your nephew for over the past ten years. As you may or may not know, the Federal Government, the IRS, the SEC and the Justice Department seized all of Darrel's assets and his wife, Sara's, assets. Sara is nowhere to be found and her attorney in Minneapolis informed me that all her bank accounts, credit cards and automobiles have been seized," I explained to the stately professional.

"Mr. Herring, her problems are not my problem or my family's concern. Darrel's businesses were his concern. The Emerson Clan in these parts have no ties to the deceased. The Federal Government has no interests or claim to our family. As a sworn officer and County Coroner for the State of Minnesota, I have no knowledge of Sara's whereabouts or Darrel's earlier marriages," the well-spoken man plainly explained his opinion.

I responded by sharing more insight about the family. "Mr. Emerson, you were involved in Darrel's phony funeral scheme which did not end well for him. I was there at his viewing and at his funeral the next day. You, sir, do not have clean hands in the

Living in a Lie

matter do you? I witnessed a deceptive funeral and then Darrel was murdered and you hid the evidence when you buried him. I expect you'll deny what happened but aren't you a little curious to know who really killed Darrel?"

William became agitated with the assertions, "Mr. Herring, if you know so much, I might conclude that you had something to do with Darrel's demise. The sheriff is a long time friend and would arrest you if I called him. You are not in the Big Twin Cities. Waterville is my turf, not only am I the County Coroner, I'm a City Councilman, a Deacon in church, a lifetime resident and the uncle of the deceased. You have no standing in these parts. If I suggest your culpability in this town, you would be beaten to death before morning. I had no motive or reason. I only tried to help Darrel get free of the government's relentless pursuit of him. They were trying to find his hidden assets and take his money, charge him with fraud and tax evasion and lock him away in a federal prison forever. He earned his wealth legally and he was only trying to evade their prosecution."

I responded with some authority, "Mr. Emerson, as I told you, I was Darrel's confidant and trusted liaison in his surreptitious activities to hide his money from creditors and the courts. You cannot imagine how much he trusted me. So do not take me for a fool. I know how involved the entire Emerson Clan is wrapped up in Darrel's financial dealings."

"Oh, really," the elder orator replied.

"Sir, I know all about the Clan's shell company, Red Sky Corporation. I know how the family bankrolled Darrel's startup investments until he had enough money to begin his pyramid schemes before swindling his wealthy investors out of hundreds of millions dollars over the last fifteen years."

"Well, Mr. Herring, it seems you've done your homework."

"I'm trying to explain to you how much I do know. Your family taught Darrel how to create his bogus public images, all his fake financial documents and then helped him to destroy his investment portfolios by diverting investor funds to hidden bank accounts offshore. You were all part of his conspiracies," I recited my knowledge to get some creditability in the conversation.

"You guys 'cooked the books' to inflate Darrel's investments. He would sucker in the fish with your bait and switched out their money with phony stock that would become worthless as the family siphoned off the money," I continued my declaration.

"You're pretty smart, Mr. Herring," the funeral director replied. "Do you have anything else to say?"

I hesitated as my subconscious mind told me to 'shut the fuck up'. I was now choking on my words. I had 'spilled the beans'.

I concluded my dissertation, "Not right now."

That was the last thing I remembered before passing out.

———————

Living in a Lie

"Seth, handcuff Herring before he wakes up and put a blindfold over his eyes before the others get here," George Emerson, the family patriarch, instructed his youngest son.

"George, the guy knows where he is and who we are," William piped in. "Why bother if we are planning to kill him after he tells us where the money is?"

"Seth, when your brother, Keith, gets here, drive Herring's Jeep to the pole barn; take off the license plates, smash in the VIN number, clean out the glove box and inside the vehicle. One of you drive it out to Townsend Cliffs overlooking Sakatah Lake and run into the lake below. Make sure it breaks through the ice and sinks before you return," George instructs the families' youngest man, a retired marine.

"What if it doesn't get far enough out from the cliff to clear the rocks?" Seth questioned his dad's plan. "Dad, in the service I learned a better way. We can drive the car onto the ice, position it over the deepest water and break the ice with a couple shotgun blasts under the car. No one lives nearby to hear the gunfire. Doing it this way, guarantees that car will sink where we want. It is unlikely the car will ever be discovered in sixty feet of water. The ice will freeze over in a couple days leaving no debris."

"Ok. Get it done and then meet us at the farmhouse. Your mother's out of town for the week and we can torture Herring in the basement without drawing attention to all of our vehicles. William, bring your Econo Van up to the building so we can get

Herring out of here and close the place up before Arty comes around again," the elder farmer instructs his brother.

"Let's get moving before the other guys arrive. They know to stop by the farm without being seen in town," George claimed.

William and George dragged me from the van, pushed me down the coal chute stairway as I stumbled to stay on my feet. They then led me into a darkened room where the other Emerson men were waiting to begin their endless interrogation. George spoke slowly while everyone, including me, listened to his instructions.

"Guys, this is Mr. Herring. He has been investigating our family and Darrel's business dealings. The week before Darrel's funeral, Mr. Herring was responsible for disbursing our money from our Cayman bank accounts to various locations that Darrel had established for us. Herring was hired to bury a briefcase in Shager Park, next to Cannon Lake, the day of Darrel's viewing. In the briefcase, was one million dollars in cash and a sealed envelope with a coded message disclosing the whereabouts of our money. Darrel has been secretly hiding over a hundred million dollars from his investment deals for us for the past fifteen years," the elder man explained to the seven other men.

"As we all know, the briefcase is missing, the money is missing, the secret code is missing, we have no idea where the Cayman stash is located and Darrel is dead. It seems that Mr. Herring was the last person to see the briefcase and to witness the transfer of our Cayman money. It seems that Herring has been digging in our corporate records in Rice County. We know from Seth's investigation that Sara Emerson is missing and the Fed's have sequestered all of her assets and her business in South Dakota," the patriarch reviewed.

"We have this house until Christmas eve without being disturbed. Mr. Herring, for the next two days one of us will be with you. You will not get food, water or sleep. We will chain you to the shower wall; you'll get a cold shower every morning and every night. There's not much heat here in this cellar. I expect you'll catch a cold and possibly freeze to death. I really do not care what happens to you. Boys, if you feel inclined to beat or torture Mr. Herring during your watch, do it while he can still feel the pain. On Saturday morning, we'll dispose of his body." George spelled out his plan.

"Mr. Herring, do you wish to say anything at this time? Seth, my youngest son, who was in the Marines. He will take of care of you for the first six hours. Guys, whoever can get Herring to talk and tell us where the money is hidden, will get Darrel's share of the hundred million," the old farmer said his piece and waited.

"Mr. Herring do you have anything to tell us at this point?" William, the mortician gave me a chance to save my life.

"Yes, yes, let me explain," I responded hoping to nullify the old man Emerson's assertions even though he was quite accurate.

"I was Darrel's trusted confidant for over the past ten years. I transported millions of dollars to the Cayman accounts. If I wanted to steal money from him, I could have done so on many occasions. In his final days, I was responsible for supervising the transfer of the money as it was flown off the island to eight destinations. I was instructed to carry one briefcase back here to Minnesota and bury it in Shager Park which I diligently did. Even after knowing of Darrel's heart attack on Labor Day weekend, I did as I was instructed. I did not open the case nor did I know of any code or message," I told the men the truth without any regret.

"What else, Mr. Herring?" Keith Allen, the oldest son and a private corporate attorney from Minneapolis, questioned me.

"I did not know of Darrel's fake funeral plans or his plan to flee the country to evade the government. I do not know who took the briefcase from Shager Park. I have to wonder if one of you guys took the case after Darrel's burial. Whoever knew of his scheme would have known about the briefcase," as I tried to raze some discontent and suspicion between the men.

"It is true; I have been investigating your family after someone set fire to my town home in Bloomington. I'm also investigating Sara' disappearance. Did you guys take her?"

Harvey Emerson, the banker in town and George's brother spoke up, "So far Mr. Herring, you have not told us anything we do not already know. What haven't you told us?"

George added his thoughts, "Herring, my brother's concerns are my concerns. We all know you are hiding critical information that you will divulge before the week has ended. Seth, he's all yours until morning. We'll leave you two to talk it out after his first shower. Good night, Mr. Herring. We hope you'll be with us in the

Living in a Lie

morning. Guys, let's go upstairs for some scotch. I bought a case of Johnny Walker Red for such an occasion."

"Ok, wait a minute, guys," as I sounded the alarm for my survival. "I have more to say. Darrel hired me in 1981 to cause the death of his first wife, Susan Ann, so he could collect on her life insurance and be rid of her. She was threatening divorce and wanted a huge settlement. Darrel told me she knew too much about his investment banking business and she alluded to your family's involvement. I suspect you all know that? Right."

"Wait just a minute, Mr. Herring. Are you accusing us of killing her?" William got into my face to question me.

"Not exactly but you guys were behind Darrel in his business dealings and I'm sure you were aware of her threats. I had no reason to take her out but you guys did. Your business in swindling wealthy investors was just getting started with the Red Rover Investment Portfolio. Darrel made lots of money for the family and he began hiding the residuals in the Cayman Islands. Susan would have brought the Feds to your doorstep," I exposed more of my knowledge of the Emerson family's dealings.

"Well, Mr. Herring, you have now given us more reasons to grind you up in the manure spreader and dispose of your remains in the potato field," George explained for the benefit of the others.

"Hey, Dad, that's funny," Seth smiled and laughed a little. "We'll have to copyright the brand as Red Herring Potatoes. Instead of feeding the hogs meat and potatoes for dinner, we can feed them meat tasting potatoes."

Patrick Henry, the younger brother to George and William and a successful contractor in Lakeville, finally said something that concerned the others, "George, I did not sign on to be involved in murder. I was not informed about hiring Herring to push Susan overboard on her fateful cruise in '81. How much money did Darrel get from her life insurance? Herring, how much did you charge for your services?"

William spoke up, "Patrick, as the second oldest in the family, I and George encouraged Darrel to do something to shut the woman up. We did not know until now that Herring was hired to silence the woman. This was Herring's way not our way."

"Ok, guys, should I continue telling you what I know?" interrupting their dispute. "By the way Patrick, I was paid my usual fee of twenty-five grand. I think Darrel got over a mill' for her death. I have no idea if the family got anything. Now, I would speculate that your family has a life insurance policy on Sara Emerson. So guys, did you take her?"

I knew I was pushing my luck with this bunch of hooligans as I tried to clear up Darrel's many secrets. However, in a panic state of mind, what could I lose? It was becoming obvious that this clandestine clan had secrets among themselves. Maybe I could rattle the patriarch enough to gain my freedom.

George piped in by ending all conversations and gave his instructions, "Patrick, we'll discuss this upstairs. Seth, you are in charge. Give the guy a cold shower and maybe he'll tell you where the money is located. We'll come down in the morning."

William encouraged everyone to exit the basement, go upstairs for a nightcap and to leave Seth alone with me. I was now concerned.

I spoke cautiously, "William, isn't that Darrel's Rolex on your wrist? I thought it was buried with him,"

"Mr. Emerson, George, I beg you not to let Seth torture me. I have more information to share," I pleaded with my captures.

"Seth, give him a shower and let him freeze. Don't hit him, just talk to him all night. Be sure to keep him awake til morning." the elder instructed his son.

"Mr. Herring, how do like our well water? Isn't it nice and cold this time of the year?" George spoke as he entered into the unheated mudroom in the farmhouse cellar. "Seth, did he open up?"

"Nope, he's as stubborn as an old German. I think he might be ready to talk," the retired marine responded.

I was exhausted, freezing cold, hungry and desperate to be free from these people. My thoughts faded into a fog as my mind fumbled for some clarity. I was weak, my fingers were numb and I could not feel my toes. I lay on the floor knowing I could not stand. The night was an endless chatter as the interrogator told his war stories repeatedly keeping me awake. I now know what it feels like to be tortured. I would rather be dead but held out hoping to redeem my value to the Emersons. I had to get them to make a deal in order to save myself from their obsession.

I had two cards left to bargain with; the money in the briefcase and the code that disclosed the location of the Emerson's cache. I had no responsibility to Sara's brother, Curt, who took the briefcase, nor did I need to hide the fact that I knew where the code was stored. However, in a drowsy state of mind the only chance of survival was to spill my guts and hope that Patrick's conscience would save me.

It did not matter that these people were Christian men, pillars of society with families at home, honorable citizens with sworn allegiance to uphold the law; what mattered at this point was 'Where is their money?'

Besides, I had not cracked the code. I had no idea where the money was taken and if I did, could I get to it? It seemed obvious that I could not escape but could I negotiate my freedom?

"Mr. Herring are you ready to divulge information about the briefcase and the code that was inside?" old man Emerson was getting angrier. "You will be getting another cold shower if you do not speak. Mr. Herring, save yourself. The money is ours and we know how to decipher the code. We'll set you free if you work with us."

"What assurance do I have if I cooperate with you?" I asked with the sound of surrender. "How do I know you'll let me go?"

"Mr. Herring, I'm the patriarch of this family. What I say the others will obey," George Emerson replied.

Living in a Lie

"Ok, let me tell you what happened after Darrel's funeral in September," I gave in to my capturers.

"On my return to the Twin Cities, I stopped by Shager Park to discover the briefcase was gone. I had no idea who took it or when it was taken," I started my narrative.

"After you guys burnt down my home in Bloomington, I figured that none of you had the briefcase. If you had, why would you come after me? I fulfilled my responsibilities to Darrel and to your family," I continued my dissertation.

"As I began investigating your businesses and your many shell companies, I figured out who took the case. Couple of weeks ago, William was vacationing in Florida when at the same time Sara disappeared. After checking with the airlines, I found that she had purchased a one-way ticket to Miami and vanished after that. Darrel had confided in me that Sara had a five hundred thousand life insurance policy on him, so why would she leave that kind of cash (tax free) on the table?" My story got the Emerson's attention.

"Continue, Mr. Herring," George directed.

"The way I figure it, William knew of the briefcase in Shager Park, he knew the money and code were inside. William took Darrel's Rolex watch after he killed Darrel on Friday night, then he retrieved the briefcase. William knew he could not go after the millions that Darrel had stashed for the family, nor could he tell you guys that he was secretly involved with Sara months before Darrel's demise. That is when Sara learned of Darrel's fake funeral plans and his plans for disappearing."

"William and Sara met up in Miami a few weeks ago to figure out where the money was located. William had the code breaker and together they located the secret accounts. To avoid suspicion, William returned to Minnesota to initiate my capture, hoping that your family would kill me. He knew I did not have the briefcase and you guys would not believe me even if I begged for my life. You would kill me and dispose of my remains. I anticipate that in a few months, William will sell the mortuary and his home in Waterville eventually joining Sara in a foreign country," that was my story, hoping it would set me free before the family questioned William.

"Mr. Herring, that's quite a story. Did you dream that up last night while suffering in the cold?" the family attorney, Keith Allen, spoke up to challenge my narrative.

"Did you guys know that William took Darrel's Rolex watch before the funeral? Did you guys know that William had been seeing Sara throughout the summer? They were rendezvousing in Mankato, on Saturday nights, staying at the Holiday Inn. Did you know that William stayed at the Park Central Hotel in Miami? Coincidentally, Sara stayed in the same hotel that same week," I expounded on the few details that I had uncovered.

"Herring, if you are fabricating these accusations to save your skin, we'll skin you alive if William can convince us otherwise," George threatened as I hung by my hands, chained to a pole still freezing from last night's cold shower.

Living in a Lie

"Dad, I think we should talk to William before we believe this big shot private investigator," said John Paul, who was a CPA in Minneapolis.

"Hey guys, can I get into some warm dry clothes while you carry out your investigation? I could get pneumonia standing in the cold. How can I help you find Sara and your money if I'm dead?" I pleaded with my caretakers.

George gave his sons the okay to change my clothes and warm me up with some coffee while he and his brother, Harvey, left the farmhouse to go visit their brother at the mortuary. It was near noon and William's receptionist would be leaving for her lunch hour.

Chapter Fifteen

The Truth Shall Set You Free

"HERRING, YOU WERE RIGHT ABOUT William," George Emerson stated as he entered the farmhouse cellar where I was warming up from my chilling inquisition.

"We did not find William at his funeral home," Harvey began to recite their findings. "The receptionist said that William did not come into work this morning nor did he call."

"We went to his home searching for him and discovered his dead body hanging from the rafters in the basement. It looked like he committed suicide but George can't accept that his brother would give up so easily," Harvey went on explaining.

George anguished over his brother's death while I caught my breath. I was shocked that William felt any remorse for Darrel. I concluded that he must been involved in more ways than I suspected. My narrative was only a hunch not the truth. Evidently, he had too much guilt and needed to avoid confessing his misdeeds to the family. He could not face the shame or explain his actions. I am always surprised how my intuition, my gut feelings, reinforces the truth.

Wow, I was expecting William to call me a liar, I thought to myself while in a state of shock. I guess he was tired of living in a life of deception."

"Herring, this changes everything. We did not know about William's deception. Everyone suspected you and Sara had conspired to take our money. But it was William," the head of the family confessed.

"Mr. Emerson, this is exactly what I was trying to tell you guys last night after seeing Darrel's watch on William's arm," as I pleaded for a reprieve. "I can help you find the money and Sara, if you trust me to be your faithful private eye. I can pickup her trail in Miami. You guys do not have the street smarts and experience as I do. Remember, Darrel trusted me for over ten years."

"Well, Mr. Herring, we have an advantage over you. Arty, the Chief of Police, has not ruled out homicide in William's death. He will be looking for you until we clear you as a suspect. Matter of fact, I think we hinted to Arty that you might be on the run avoiding an arrest. He did find your parka in the mortuary and has the idea that you were the last one to see William alive."

"Okay, I can work with that provided I will be exonerated by your family when I return, with or without the money. Sara may have grabbed the money and fled to another part of the world. If she has, by the time I track her down, she may be gone again. How long should I search for her and the money before returning?" I responded but did not like the terms. How in the hell can I transfer a hundred million dollars to the Emersons in Minnesota without detection?

"I will need some transportation to the Twin Cities and money to cover expenses," was my plea.

"Herring, you can take the funeral home's Econo Van and leave it in a parking lot somewhere in Minneapolis; eventually the cops will find it; trace it back here; call Arty and he'll assume you used it to escape. I'll have Seth retrieve the vehicle later," the cagey old farmer instructed.

"As far as your expenses are concerned, look at this assignment as your last one if you do not find that woman. Spend some of the money Darrel paid you. If you are successful, we'll give you Darrel's share and William's share. The way I figure it, it might be more than twenty million. It's worth it. Right?" George Emerson presented his last offer to me.

"I'll need my wallet, my credit cards, the keys to the van and a warm coat for the drive," conceding to their demands with many reservations.

The men took off the handcuffs and gave me a coat along with the keys to the van.

"You had better take off, Herring. I know that Arty and the County Sheriff are still investigating the crime scene at William's house. An APB has not been issued yet. Good luck Mr. Herring. We'll give you thirty days before I call the FBI and tell them about Darrel's first wife's death," old man Emerson motioned for me to leave the farmhouse.

———————

I was exhausted, hungry and freezing as I drove away from that crazy little farm town, hoping to never return. I could hardly stay awake but I knew the cops would be searching for me before nightfall. I needed to get back to Minneapolis, sneak into my condo in the Towers, pack a bag, grab eight grand, get to my storage garage in the warehouse district, retrieve my van with Iowa license plates and get out of the state before the Feds started looking for me.

The hour and thirty-minute drive gave me time to think about where Sara might be. I knew her and Darrel had a condo in Mexico but I figured the Feds knew that as well. If she flew to Miami, where would she go from there? Did she know the location of the hundred million dollars? Would she try to take it?

Chapter Sixteen

Red Sky

IT TOOK THREE DAYS TO drive to Miami without anyone knowing of my trip or destination. I did not want to leave a paper trail with the airlines or with my credit cards. I had enough cash to last the month only if I bought just the necessities during my hunt for Sara. I had no idea if she had any cash but I knew she was smart enough not to use credit cards to avoid the Feds from tracking her.

During the drive, I had plenty of time to explore all the possibilities of where Sara might be hiding, that is if she was still in Florida. Wherever she might be, I knew she would be near or staying near the wealthiest communities in Southern Florida. My first guess was West Palm Beach where Darrel's daughter, Susan, had a town home on the ocean.

Finding the posh home was easy. Darrel always stayed in the home while having his sexual escapades. I remembered tracking him to the exact location last summer for Sara. I anticipated that Susan Emerson was able to keep the expensive home as part of a deal with the Feds for testifying against her stepmother and her father's estate.

I did not expect to find Sara at the Emerson family hideaway. However, Darrel's daughter might be able give me some ideas of where I might find her stepmother.

As I arrived in the Miami area, I decided to go directly to Susan's exclusive home on North Ocean Boulevard hoping to find her before nightfall.

I parked on the street a block away and walked cautiously towards the house looking for the cops or the Feds that might be watching for me. There were many high priced vehicles parked in driveways near the exclusive homes. Fortunately, none of them looked like cop cars or government cars. I did not feel safe approaching the driveway to the luxury, three-story stucco home. I rang the doorbell with caution not knowing who would open the door.

I waited. Rang the bell a second time and then again. Finally, I could see someone through the stained glass sidelight approaching the main door. The door opened. There in the afternoon sun was a goddess from Neptune, standing in a two-piece bathing suit with long glowing blonde hair.

I knew Emerson's daughter was attractive from seeing her at her father's funeral but I did not envision her in a bikini with a golden tan.

I was taken by surprised and appeared speechless when she asked, "Who are you and how can I help you?"

"Miss, I'm sorry to intrude and for not calling ahead. My name is Redmond Herring. I was a business associate of your father's. I did a lot of private business for him. I was employed by him for over ten years," I could barely talk while examining this beautiful specimen of a perfect woman.

"Why are you here? You must know that my father died in September. I'm not involved in his past nor in any of the lawsuits he left behind. Matter of fact, Mr. Herring, I'm rather upset that you interrupted my afternoon yoga session. I'm paying my instructor by the hour. We just got started. If you wish to wait until I am finished, I'll be kind enough to take a few minutes to talk you. Please come in and help yourself to a cool drink in the frig. I'll be outside on the deck."

"Thank you, I will not cause any problems. Thanks for the drink," I replied showing respect for her privacy.

I was content to sit in the living room area while watching two beautiful women stretching and gyro flexing their bodies on the outside deck overlooking the Atlantic Ocean. It was like watching two mermaids swimming in sync. I would have to thank old man Emerson, Susan's grandfather, for freeing me to begin my search in Florida.

Living in a Lie

"Mr. Herring, thank you for your patience. Can you wait a little longer so I may shower and change clothing?" Darrel Emerson's oldest of two daughters kindly excused herself as she sauntered up the open staircase to the third floor.

I greeted the yoga instructor, "goodbye," as the tall thin muscular female closed the main entrance door, leaving me alone with a twenty-four year old voluptuous diva.

As I waited for the Minnesota princess to come down the stairway, I walked out to the deck remembering that memorable night last summer when I watched her father flounder in front of the fireplace with two erotic black women.

"Mr. Herring, I remember you were at my father's funeral commiserating with my stepmother, Sara, during the burial service. You should know that I do not like Sara. She was my dad's third wife after my maternal mother died in 1981 and my dad divorced his second wife in 1991," the goddess spoke while descending from the upper level, barefoot, wearing a pure white silk jump suit as her long hair trailed behind her sensuous body.

"I do remember that sad day in Waterville. I knew Sara a few years before she married your father," I reluctantly responded not to divulge any solidarity with Sara. I needed Susan's insights and cooperation for tracking down her stepmother.

"Mr. Herring, may I call you Redmond?" She began her investigation.

"Miss Emerson, may I call you Susan?" I smartly replied. "You can call me Red."

"Red, so what brings you here to my doorstep? I hope my dad did not owe you money. After his funeral, the Feds took just about everything from our family and from Sara. If it weren't for my personal savings and investments, I would not be able to stay here in West Palm Beach," as she apologized for her meager existence.

"Susan, I'm here on behalf of your relatives in Waterville. Your granddad, George, hired me to investigate Sara's business concerns before the Feds find her. The family believes Sara is hiding a large sum of their investment money. They want me to get it back before it is gone," I carefully exposed part of my mission.

"Why would you stop here in West Palm Beach? Sara would never contact me," young Ms. Emerson replied.

"Susan, I'm really getting hungry. How about we go to your favorite restaurant for dinner; I'll buy. Maybe we can help each other resolve some of those questions surrounding your father and his business dealings," I was encouraging the woman to keep our dialogue going.

"Sure, I must warn you, I'm not a hearty eater. My choice of dining may not be yours," she clarified her dietary habits. "I'm a

Living in a Lie

vegetarian. My dad always insisted on eating somewhere else, for a heavier meal. Are you sure, Mr. Herring?"

"Whatever you like. I'm sure I can submit to your desires," that was my first sexual innuendo for the evening.

"Red, are you married?" she inquired with some interests.

"No and I'm not considering it in the near future," I replied with a smile catching a possible hint of where I would be sleeping for the night.

"Again, Mr. Herring, I must warn you that I prefer being with older men," the tempting young woman took the bait.

It was near midnight when we finally returned to Susan's home after having dinner, drinks and lively conversations. She had many fascinating stories to share about the Emerson relatives. She admitted to having many indiscretions with her father's brothers in Waterville, when visiting the farm as a young high school girl.

This exotic woman explained that she got her sexual education behind grandpa's barn, beginning at the young age of twelve.

If I had only known last week when those bullies were torturing me in her granddad's basement, I might have had some advantage in countering their threats.

Oh well, what was now in store for me would be dispensed by another Emerson descendant, hopefully without any pain or suffering.

Again, I would have to thank old man Emerson for letting me come to Florida.

As the Phoenix closed the front door and locked the deadbolt, I experienced the most hedonistic sexual encounter while my clothing was being torn from my body. I felt like a fresh tomato being eaten by a starving vegan. My flesh turned red as her teeth scraped over my skin. Her French kisses were erotic and passionate as if she had never been sexually satisfied. Wild, untamed and feral like a hungry animal escaping from a cage. I thought I had been tortured last week. This vixen needed a cold shower.

Whew.

When I awoke from a self-inflicted blackout, all I could remember was blonde hair flying in all directions. Finally, what seemed like hours, the lioness passed out from exhaustion, saving me from having a heart attack.

I was lying in her bed wondering how many older men had been devoured and found dead in her bed. I had no recollection of anything after my clothing was ripped from body. I have no idea if I even enjoyed this fervent episode.

When I found the energy to get up, I realized I was alone in a third floor bedroom. I staggered down the hall to the top landing of the open staircase to see Susan swimming nude in the outdoor pool, basking in morning sunlight.

I smelled breakfast awaiting my hungry appetite as we met in the kitchen area, kissing briefly. A white shear silk robe covered her beautiful body as I stood there in red and blue plaid shorts. Not quite the scene one would find in a GQ Magazine.

"Sweetheart, that was an awesome, unforgettable evening. Thank you for having mercy in the end. I could've died," my comments broke the air of silence while I smiled with contentment.

"Red, I'm happy you stayed the night. I was hungry for passion and eager to taste a Minnesota man," she replied while handing a tray full of food, directing me to sit at the table on the outside deck.

It was below zero back in Minnesota but seventy-five degrees in Florida. Thank you, Mr. Emerson.

Later that morning, I left Susan's home to begin checking out various banks in Miami. I went to all the banks Darrel visited in May and I was hoping to pickup Sara's trail starting at the Park Central Hotel. After spending most of the day searching for clues, I realized I would have to go back to the Cayman Islands and question the bankers that transferred Darrel's cache into those eight cases.

Meanwhile, I expected that Susan called her granddad in Minnesota to check me out. When I returned to her luxury home, she seemed more attentive, respectful and cooperative. I'm sure the family patriarch told her to stay close by and help me find Sara Emerson.

"Susan, I need to get to the Cayman Islands without detection and without showing my passport to US Officials. Could you recommend a charter service for leasing a yacht? I would need a captain and crew," I questioned the diva as I entered her beachfront home.

"Red, I have a friend who will let me take out his forty foot, Schucker Motorsailer. I'll call him and ask him. How long will we be gone?" Susan asked for more details.

"I would like to get into George Town just before dark, anchor in the harbor for the night and go ashore for a day. We will need a captain, I'm not familiar with blue water sailing," I replied with some apprehension. "My guess, a couple of days."

"Well, Red, you underestimate my abilities. I have been sailing in the ocean for over ten years with my dad. Every time he came to Florida for business, we would charter a different yacht. I got my captain's certificate for forty-footers years ago. I'm Coast Guard Certified as a navigator with instruments and with a sexton," the over competent woman replied with pride.

"Really. I did not know that," I was surprised with her accomplishments.

"Redmond, I do not want to brag too much. However, I can sail most single mast sloops and ketches with fore and aft rigging, solo. If you have your 'sea legs', I would appreciate your help with the sails. You must agree that I'm the captain and follow my orders," the mystery woman asserted your confidence.

"Whatever you want. I can take orders; did I not submit to your commands last night?" I replied with a wink.

Living in a Lie

"Call your friend. I'd like to leave tomorrow, if possible. We'll need to go shopping for supplies this evening," encouraging the diva to execute our plans.

"Redmond, I'll see if we can board his yacht tonight and sail at sunup," the self-appointed captain replied.

Our plans worked out perfectly as we loaded our provisions into the large sailboat called, 'Red Sky', before dining at a local marina restaurant. We enjoyed the fine wines, a seafood medley of grouper and lobster, laughing and laughing at our 'Ole and Lena' jokes, which only Minnesota natives would understand. She was born and raised in Bloomington, Minnesota, moving to Florida during the summer of 1990.

It must have been near nine o'clock when we walked down the boardwalk to our floating waterbed. I was anticipating the captain would order her deckhand to her master suite for late evening directives on how to see Venus while holding a sexton. Right on... I'm all for late night commands.

We were standing on the dock near the yacht when she noted, "We have a red sky tonight. That means good sailing tomorrow. We need to get a good night's sleep and leave port early. As soon as we board the ship, I will need your help in securing all the hatches while I check all the mooring lines."

All night, the boat was rocking side to side. I could not tell if was the tide or the activities in the captain's quarters.

I have always enjoyed waking onboard a yacht, no matter where it was harbored. As the early morning sun appears over the quiet harbor, one can hear the seagulls chirping with delight as they dive into the calm waters searching for small fishes near the surface.

Sleeping in a marina with hundreds of sailboat halyards banging on their masts, can be a hardship for a novice. For me, it was a pleasant sound to my ears after Susan finally went to sleep. The sounds in a harbor seemed to calm my soul.

It was 0700 when I rolled out of bed; I went to the head, wandered through the galley before climbing upstairs through the hatchway to find the captain sitting on the foredeck, drinking herbal tea.

"Red, it's about time you got your ass on deck. We need to ready the sails, fire up the inboard, check the fuel, calibrate the compass and test the radio, radar and sonar. After we set sail away from the shoals, you can make breakfast while I navigate to set our course for the Cayman Island," her orders were loud and clear.

I was now under the control of an over enthusiastic captain, in a hurry to start my day with a sip of coffee. My head was pounding with pain from the last night's pleasures. How in the world did I permit this vibrant woman to control my destiny for the next couple of days?

"Red, as I power up the engine you can untie the lines from the dock, push off the bow and then jump aboard as the stern clears the dock," the mean and ugly captain yelled out her forceful orders.

"Aye, aye captain," her first mate moaned.

"Hey, Red, get moving or I'll leave you behind. Hurry up, jump aboard, secure the fenders, take up the dock lines and stow them in aft hatch. Be careful not to fall overboard," her orders were loud and confusing for this novice sailor.

"Hey, captain, is it time for a bloody Mary yet. I think I'm getting seasick. Can we turn around and charter an airplane?" I groaned with pain.

"Red, get with it, sailor. You need to unfurl the main sail, now. After I set course, you'll have to untie the jib and winch it up. Hurry; there is no time to fret. Be sure to snap on your safety lines. Where's your life jacket, sailor?" her commands were unrelenting as I felt pain in my hamstrings.

"Captain, madam, Susan, Ms. Emerson, give me some slack, I'm not one those young taut sailors you been boating with," I was trying to get some sympathy from the wench.

"Herring, man up and get back here to the cockpit and take the wheel while I check the instruments and our course," she ordered.

Our 830 mile journey would take two days with seasonal winds blowing us at an average speed of twenty knots. We would be sailing in the Straits of Florida into the Gulf of Mexico with our first port of call, Havana Harbor, at the marina in Casablanca, Cuba.

We would spend the night, anchored in the harbor while staying onboard. At sunup, we would sail westward off the northern coast of Cuba, navigating into the Caribbean Sea and then south, southeast to the Cayman Islands, hoping to arrive late on the second day, before nightfall.

After listening to our confidant captain plot a course on the charts, I affirmed my fears; I should have flown. It would have been faster, safer and easier on my aching muscles. What the hell, here I am with a beautiful twenty-four year old nymphomaniac, sailing towards the blue waters of the romantic Caribbean Sea, in route to retrieve the Emerson's fortune of one hundred million dollars. Maybe we should spend a couple of days laying on beach and making love in the midnight moonlight before returning to reality.

———————

The northeastern winds were blowing us south at thirty knots making the experience rather challenging for me. However, Captain Emerson was thrilled to be clipping along faster than she anticipated. If the prevailing winds continued, we would be rounding the Key West Islands two hours ahead of schedule. This was great as I was getting bored seeing nothing but water. We could not navigate too close to the coast, concerned for the shoal line and coral reefs.

This Neptune goddess was excited while under sail with so much exuberance. I was not happy after being distraught with seasickness, never wanting to taste seafood again. I was thankful for the tropical breeze that cooled our bodies as we worked the sails in our bathing suits.

The first leg of our journey went fast, as the captain pointed to the northern coastline of Cuba, which we then followed for about two hours until our port of call; Havana, Cuba appeared while the sun was setting in the western skies.

That night in Havana Harbor, we anchored in a 'safe-harbor zone.' There was no amorous play between us; one of us always had to stand watch in two-hour shifts, to prevent unwanted intruders from boarding on ship.

———————

Sunrise came earlier. Captain Emerson was anxious to leave the unsavory mooring before anyone noticed our luxury yacht. As we motored out to sea, I prepared the main sail, stored away the fenders and sail covers, while the captain plotted her course.

The second day of our voyage we had twenty-two knot winds blowing across our bow from the northwest, the Gulf of Mexico, causing us to lay onto the port side as we skimmed across the blue ocean. The temperature was in the nineties as the wind cooled our skin.

Four hours into our journey, the captain yelled out a new order, "Prepare to come about."

The main sail and the jib began to flutter as the ship took a sharp left to the port side; the beam almost knocked me overboard as it blew across the deck stretching the halyards until the winches eased the tension, holding the wind in our sails. The mainsail opens on the starboard and jib to the port. She called this is 'jybing the jib' as the wind blew at us squarely and both sails bellowed to their fullest stretch.

It was quite a show watching this wild woman take control of the wild beast as we changed our course to south-southeast. She was very skilled at handling the maneuver without any assistance from her tender crew.

I was impressed and still onboard, standing near the helm as 'Red Sky' slowed to twelve knots.

Now that was exhilarating.

"Hey, captain, why are we going slower?" I asked her with some concern.

"When heading southeast with the wind blowing from the northwest, I have chosen to square off rather then tacking back and forth. It is slower but we will do this for about an hour and then change our course to eastward. Tacking would actually take us longer," Ms. Emerson explained.

I had no idea what that meant but she knew where we were headed and how to get there.

———————

All afternoon I sat watching the horizon looking for an island in the middle of nowhere. The sun was hot and directly above as we neared the equator. There was a light breeze blowing across the deck making life bearable but still boring.

It was near 1800 hours (6:00 PM), when we sailed into the leeward side of the Cayman Island as our sails went silent and still. The captain turned the engine on while ordering her first mate to drop the sails, layout the fenders and ready the dock lines, as we headed into a nearby harbor.

I concluded that these experiences of sailing in the blue waters 'were moments of terror followed by hours of boredom.' The next time I travel to any island in the ocean, I will definitely charter an airplane.

George Town is a unique city existing on a 22-mile long coral reef, 200 miles south of Cuba, in the middle of the Caribbean Sea with a population of 25,000.

There are ten private banks on this island, which guaranteed complete privacy for their customers, all because of this sovereign country's national privacy and tax free laws.

Darrel Emerson took advantage of these laws to hide his fortune from the United States Government, avoiding detection and US taxes. He embezzled more the one hundred million dollars from his bogus frauds and phony investments. As his confidant, I transported millions of dollars of cash to be deposited in nine secret bank accounts throughout the 80's.

Here I was, years later, trying to recapture all that money, traveling with Darrel's twenty-four year old daughter, under the direction of the Emerson Family patriarch, avoiding the FBI, SEC and the US Justice Department.

I must be insane to think I could get away with my plan while the family loyalist was scrutinizing all my activities. I had no way of knowing the outcome of this treasure hunt. Personally, I concluded that the money was still on the island; in one of Darrel's nine accounts, he had created as a ruse to conceal his stash. His family only knew of the eight accounts and eight transfers.

In all of my trips, I made sure to note all nine banks and account numbers for Darrel's deposits. I intended to keep track of his money, until eight couriers flew the money elsewhere. As far as I could tell, no one knew of my secret safe-deposit box hidden in another bank.

The main concern was how could I retrieve the account numbers without Susan Emerson discovering my hidden bank account?

Living in a Lie

Captain Emerson piloted our ship into the Barcadere Marina, the oldest barcadere in the Cayman Islands. The harbormaster directed us to our slip.

We secured the 'Red Sky,' showered separately, mainly because most showers on boats are small and cramped without enough room for an extra towel.

I dressed for dinner in a white cotton shirt and cotton pants wearing open sandals. The goddess barely covered herself with a white silk strapless blouse, without a bra, while wearing a very short white silk skirt with white sandals.

A cool breeze swirled over the small island, the sun was setting as we walked on cobblestone streets to a nearby nightclub. Most of the patrons were boaters traveling the southern seas. The locals dined in their homes hoping that the tourists would boost the economy.

After dinner and too much wine, we returned to our floating abode to share an amaretto with Irish Cream on ice. That magic aphrodisiac accelerated our amorous play. My sexual appetite trumped the young woman when she finally passed out, exhausted from a day of sailing.

Caribbean morning skies are unforgettable, most often glowing with yellow and orange rays of sun reflecting off the deep aqua blue waters of the sea, as fresh and pure air kept the island cool until midday.

"Susan, it is midmorning and time to wake up," I whisper in her ear not wanting to startle the damsel.

"Red, can you go ashore and pick up some hot tea and coffee and maybe bring me a scone or bagel? I want to sleep for an hour or so," the tired captain moaned.

"Will do, captain," respecting her wishes hoping to sneak away to my bank to retrieve the hidden bank account numbers.

Fortunately, the bank was only a couple of blocks away from the marina and had opened early. I darted in, presented my account number and asked to access my safe-deposit box.

I was absent from the boat for less than an hour returning with some coffee, warm tea and bagels when Ms Emerson questioned my whereabouts, "Red, where have you been? I'm hungry and I've been waiting for you."

"Good morning, captain. I went for a short walk and brought back bagels and your hot tea," I replied quickly to deflect any more questions.

Chapter Seventeen

Sailor Take Warning

"RED, WHILE YOU ARE TAKING a shower and getting dressed, I'm going into the village for groceries and supplies. I'll cook a special dinner for you tonight. You have been a fairly good crew and deserve to relax and let me feed your Minnesota appetite," the diva expressed her plans.

"Okay, when I finish I'll meet you at the Grand Old House for a light lunch. I'll rent a car for the day," I wanted to oblige her, anticipating she would call Minnesota to check in with her granddad.

The weather seemed to be changing as the warm southern winds gave way to a cooler breeze blowing in from the northeast. The locals were always aware of the weather conditions knowing that any change would affect tourism on the island.

I had the list of eight banks where we had to interview the bank officers. The first banker looked through their records and told us what I already knew. The account was closed on September 6, 1993.

Susan was watching my every move. She did not speak while I questioned the other bank officers. The president at the eighth bank recognized me and then caught me off guard in front of my cohort while she was staring at me, "Mr. Herring, I remember you. Mr. Emerson told me your name and instructed me to sign over that locked aluminum case when you arrived in my bank on September 6. Matter of fact, I have the signed release here in the file," he handed me the document. Ms. Emerson asked to inspect the receipt.

Only Darrel and I knew about the ninth account and the ninth withdrawal and I was not about to tell anyone or go into that bank, which also held my personal accounts.

After we examined all of Darrel's bank account records, I called old man Emerson in Minnesota to report the unfortunate news. There was no money in any of the banks. No leads to where Darrel had transferred the money. I would return to Miami and begin my search elsewhere.

I expected Susan would call her grandfather to report the same information as well.

"Red, I need to make a call to my family. Please drop me off at the marina office before you return the rental car. I'll see you at the boat," the impoverished heir instructed.

I was sitting on the foredeck, sipping some coffee waiting for the captain to return. When I saw her walking down the pier towards the boat, she looked upset and distraught.

"Mr. Herring, why did we come here if you already knew my dad had transferred the money elsewhere? My grandfather is upset for wasting a week on this boondoggle. If there wasn't money here in the Cayman Islands, why do you think that Sara or anyone would come here?" she inquired with anger.

At first, I did not respond. I needed to think about my answer. "Susan, excuse me for dragging you here but I did not know your father had closed the accounts. I figured he only removed part of the money. How could I have known? The cases were locked when I took possession of them. I did what I was told. The Emerson family knew that. Matter of fact, they knew I hid the last case near Cannon Lake for one of your relatives to retrieve," I became defensive at her assertions and accusations.

"Red, we're leaving for Miami in the morning. I do not feel like making dinner tonight. This entire ordeal has upset me. I'm not going to be very good company so you should probably go into town and eat dinner alone," Susan stepped aboard the yacht, went below and closed the hatch without saying anything else.

Wow, I did not see that coming. The woman is pissed. I'll have to apologize to her in the morning. As I recalled, she offered to sail me to the islands without hesitation. I knew she wanted to get her hands on the money. However, I did not promise anyone anything. I came here looking for Sara.

I walked down the dock towards land, headed over to the marina restaurant for some food and noticed the clouds blowing in from the north. I was always told that when cool air mixes with hot air, rain would follow. I worried about the change of weather not seeing a red sky in the western horizon.

It was near 1100 hours when I stepped onto the deck, slid the hatch door open to the main saloon and then retired into the aft cabin for the night. It was lonely and cold without Susan's hot body near me.

As I lay in the bunk trying to get some sleep, my thoughts of the past two weeks kept gnawing at my intuition.

"Mr. Herring, get your ass on deck, now. We must hurry to begin sailing to the west before the storm makes landfall. Ready the sails; take in the dock lines and the fenders; stow them here in the aft compartment. Do not raise the jib. The winds will be heavy until the rain passes," the captain was up and ready to take command of my life, forevermore.

As our voyage began, the captain began to question the many assignments her father had for me in the 80s. I then noticed the red sky in the eastern sunrise as we headed west by northwest towards

Living in a Lie

Mexico. Her questions took on an angry tone while investigating her father's activities of the past twelve years.

We were clipping along at 20 knots without the jib. The weather was now blowing us to the north by northwest as the cold rain caught up to us drenching our clothing. There was no time to put on rain gear with waves heaving the craft 10 feet up and then plummeting down into the deep chasms crashing into the next wave.

This was not what I was hoping for as the vixen struggled with a loose line, pulling it into a winch, securing it to a cleat while holding the wheel as steady as she could.

"What can I do? How can I help?" I screamed for her guidance.

"Red, you'll have to go forward to the main mast and lower the sail before it rips out the rivets. Hurry," she yelled at me.

I held onto the deck rails with all of my strength, edging forward trying to get a hold of the mast as the boat began heaving up and over another high wave, nose diving into the next.

The heavy winds shifted to the starboard and the main beam swung across the deck slamming me overboard. In all the panic, I had not attached my safety lines nor was I wearing a lifejacket.

"Susan, throw me a line, throw me the ring, help me," I screamed as loud as I could.

"Redmond Herring, you son of bitch, you now know how my mother felt after you pushed her off the cruise ship in 1981. This is almost the same reckoning of her drowning. Goodbye, Mr.

Herring," the wicked witch of the deep blue sea laughed while I was treading water and gasping for air.

I felt like a drowning fish floundering to survive.

The waves were whipping me around like a bobber just before the weight of my body pulls me underwater. Here I was, trying to stay afloat, hoping to live for another day.

"Hey there sailor, do you need help?" I recognized the voice that was yelling at me from a large motor yacht floating nearby. It was Sara Blake. How in the hell did she find me?

"Sara," I yelled in a panic. "Is that you my dearest friend? How in the hell did you find me?"

"Red, knowing what I know about you, I anticipated finding you in a bar smoking a Cuban cigar in George Town. I should let you swim back to Miami along with all the other sharks. I assume all sharks like eating red herrings," she laughed while throwing me a life ring with an attached line.

"Sara, get me aboard. I have a lot to tell you," struggling to get onto the swim platform at the rear of a huge yacht.

"Okay, Mr. Herring, only if you promise to share your new found wealth with me. I never want to be an impoverished widow ever again," the smitten woman handed me a towel as I climbed onto the main deck.

Exhausted, cold and wet, I wanted to get out of the fierce rain and heavy winds. If it were not for this mysterious woman, I would be gasping my last breath before drowning in the deep waters of the ocean.

"Sara, we need to turn around and return to the Cayman Islands before anyone finds out where Darrel hid his money. I know where it is," I did not want Susan Emerson to find it. We can retrieve the fortune together," I insisted she listen to me.

After Sara gave instructions to the captain, the sixty-foot motor yacht circled around to set a new course back to the Cayman Islands, headed directly into the storm.

"Sara, tell me how you found me in the middle of the ocean, in the middle of a rain storm. I'm also curious to know what are you doing in the Caribbean? When did you leave Minnesota? Why did you leave?" My questions challenged her presence.

"Red, I left Minnesota to avoid prosecution by the Feds. They sequestered everything including my business, my finances, my Jaguar and my home. I had to get away from it all. My mother has my kids in her custody," she cried as her loneliness tempered her emotions.

"I flew to Miami to meet up with an old friend and I hid out in the Park Central Hotel for a week before chartering a yacht to the Cayman Islands. I have a secret safe-deposit box in one of the banks where I have been stashing money for a rainy day. I guess that day has come. I was making plans to travel back to the mainland when I saw you and my stepdaughter coming into harbor the other day, near where my charter was tied up. I've been watching you two from that moment," she explained.

"Sara, the old friend you met in Miami, was that William Emerson by chance?" I asked her causally not to upset her. She was still my guardian angel and I did not want be thrown overboard ever again.

"How did you know that, Red?" she quickly responded.

"I sort of got tangled up with the Emerson Clan in Waterville after William returned to Minnesota. How long have you been involved with Darrel's uncle? It's really none of my business," I was avoiding eye contact with the scarlet.

"I've been seeing William, on and off, since I was seventeen, soon after my sister was shot by my younger brother, back in 1967. William started mentoring and counseling me through my grief and loss. He has been the only person that ever reached out to me until I met Morgan Blake. I did not have much contact with William until after I left the farm in 1989. After you and I broke up in 1991, I called William; he knew I was involved with Darrel and needed to talk. We met at the Thunderbird Hotel in Bloomington and finally consummated our lifelong love for each other. No one ever knew," Sara cried with sadness in her heart.

"I could never tell Darrel and I knew I broke William's heart when I married his nephew," she wept more.

"William told me that the family was searching for Darrel's millions that were stashed in an offshore account in the Cayman Islands. I never knew he had money hidden away but it did not surprise me. William had a copy of the code that my brother gave to me, subsequently, I gave it to you. Remember? Did you ever crack the code, Red?" Sara continued telling her saga.

"No, I did not figure it out so I went to Waterville hoping to find more clues. Did he ever find out who really killed his nephew? Did you tell him?" I was hoping to get some hints from the mystifying vixen.

"No, I did not tell him. William was the one helping Darrel evade capture and escape prosecution. The Emerson family men wanted to get their hands on the offshore money before the government found it. When William called and wanted to be together in Florida, I agreed and left Minnesota without telling anyone, including you, mainly because I knew the Feds were tracking me.

While at the Park Central, we solved the code and deciphered Darrel's last message to his family. It was not good news motivating William to return to Waterville, immediately," her narrative completed the puzzle.

The heavy seas were rough on my stomach as the ship pitched over the high waves. I needed to find the head promptly. After returning to the main saloon, I found Sara waiting wrapped in a beach blanket to stay warm.

"Sara, do you have Darrel's letter?" hoping she had it with her.

"Here you go, Red. It's not good for the clan," she took an envelope out of her beach bag purse and handed it to me to read.

The letter read... *To my family: Dad, Uncle William, Uncle Harvey and to my four brothers. All I wanted was to live a simple life in Waterville but*

*you all influenced me to go to college. You pushed
me to succeed beyond my capabilities, forcing me
to lie, cheat, steal and even murder my first wife,
in order to meet your expectations and protect
our assets. I became your puppet, while you guys
enjoyed a debt free lifestyle, at my expense.*

*When I was a young boy, you spent time teaching
us boys (not how to fish) but the art of "fishing". You
taught us how to create false pretenses, facades,
illusions of grandeur and what bait to use to catch
big fish. The only reason I went to college was
to please my dad in his plans for me to begin
networking (fishing) for wealthy kids. You taught
me the only reason a 'farm boy from Minnesota'
would join a country clubs in the big cities, is for
fishing. Everyone but me, enjoy my wealth. I spent
it all searching for peace and happiness. I've been
unhappy living a false life. There is no money. Fuck
you all.*

"Wow, I'm shocked. I cannot imagine how the Emerson clan must have felt after reading this," voicing some sympathy to my dear friend.

"Red, William did not take the letter to his family. He told me to keep it private and hidden," she explained.

Living in a Lie

"Sara, I must tell you some sad news. William hung himself the week he returned to Minnesota. He left no letter and did not tell the family," I tried to console her knowing she loved William.

"My heartaches for the Emerson family. I suppose I should send Darrel's letter to George, to help him understand how his greed killed his favorite son and his brother," she cried with sorrow and heartbreak for all that had happened.

"How in the world did you discover that long message from a paragraph of mismatched words on that coded sheet of paper?" I was perplexed.

"Darrel gave his uncle William a sealed envelope before staging his fake funeral, just in case something went wrong. In the envelope was the clue needed for solving the code, which was in the briefcase left near Cannon Lake. William contacted me to see if you had taken the code out of the briefcase before hiding it. I told him you took the code and gave it to me to keep it," the vixen told her story.

"Why would you tell him that? That's why the family was so upset with me," my anger began to show.

"Red, I could not implicate my brother. The Emerson family would hunt him down and kill him. He is family, you know."

Sara continued telling her story, "William instructed me to meet him in Florida and bring the code. He wanted to find the money and leave the country so he and I could live somewhere else in the world."

"So you threw me to the wolves without telling me? You left me hanging in limbo wondering where you were. You completely vanished. I thought maybe the Feds incarcerated you until they could file charges and convict you of fraud. I was worried for you, calling everyone. You could have contacted me, Sara," I pleaded my concerns and expressed my frustration with the entire mess.

"Red, I'm sorry. I knew you could survive the government's scrutiny and the Emerson family's revenge. I could not. So when William offered me a new life, I had no choice," she began crying, wanting me to hold her.

"Damn it, Sara. I have no idea what will happen now. In all my days as a confidant and PI, I have never, ever, met such a selfish. self-centered, narcissistic, lying woman like you. You have used me, abused me, lied to me and accused me, endangering my life for your own well-being," my anger finally lashed out at the indignant woman.

At that moment, Sara placed her soft hands on my face and asked for my forgiveness. She was weeping in sorrow, apologizing for her selfish actions.

I gave up my soul when she kissed my lips. She knew how to disarm my anger.

"Red, please forgive me. Let me remind you, I just saved you from drowning. Together, we can get Darrel's money out of the Cayman bank and go live in Australia forever. I promise I'll love you until I die. This is what we both deserve," Sara pleaded.

The captain navigated the yacht out of the rain and heavy storms while Sara and I sat holding each other quietly. He yelled to us from the upper deck, "We should be in the Cayman Islands by nightfall. From here to there, the waters will be smooth and the sun will be warm."

I was exhausted from my near death experience and from listening to Sara's endless plight for a better life. We slept holding each other for the entire trip back to George Town.

I had had a feeling Sara was in George Town. I did not see her but my intuition led me to think about her whereabouts. I'm sure when she heard Darrel had hidden millions in the Cayman Islands she would find her way to the fortune.

We arrived at 1800 hours and woke as our ship maneuvered into the harbor. I asked Sara, "Is your bank account in RBC (Royal Bank of Canada)?"

"How did you know that?" she seemed surprised.

"Sara, I went into RBC Wednesday, midmorning to withdraw money from my private account. As I opened the lobby doors, I smelled your distinctive perfume. I would know that fragrance anywhere. Then again, that evening, I went to the marina restaurant for a sandwich and picked up your scent. I had no idea where you were staying but I noticed the only other ship in the marina, the 'Dream On' had a port of call for 'Miami, Florida'," I explained my receptive senses.

"Red, I could never fool you. I followed you and Susan in a taxi Wednesday afternoon to each of the eight banks. I watched as you both came out of the banks unhappy without anything in your hands. I concluded you discovered what I already knew. Darrel's offshore bank accounts were closed in September. There wasn't any money to be found," Sara admitted her undercover investigation.

The captain and crew prepared dinner for us as the red sun disappeared into the red horizon. We finished our dinner; the crew took leave and went ashore while we retired to the lower deck, finding our way to the main saloon, which had a couple bottles of wine needing our attention.

It seems that every time Sara and I resumed our passion, the lovemaking got better. The Minnesota goddess would again, land on her feet gaining momentum in her quest to be rich. I hope that this time we will be in concert.

Friday, December 31, 1993

Sara woke up as the warm sunlight began shining through the starboard port lights proclaiming a new day for the small Caribbean island. She was anxious to uncover her deceased husband's secret stash of money. There was no chance I could sleep any longer or expect any sexual favors from my playmate.

"Red, wake up and let's have breakfast and go find the money," she encouraged me to sit up and face our destiny.

"Sara, the money will still be in the bank when we get to it," I mumbled while staggering into the head.

I dressed slowly while she scurried out of the saloon to make her appearance on the main deck, ordering the captain to serve up her morning delight. Fresh fruit plate with an open pineapple, tomato juice with a freshly baked scone.

As I arrived on deck, I surveyed the calm waters in the harbor; noticing the locals on shore preparing their wares for merchandizing to the tourist. Everything on the island was over priced; in short supply, and rare; including the ingredients for a bloody Mary.

Freighters arrived weekly with new supplies restocking stores, restaurants and homes. I was glad the captain had a private stash of tomato juice and vodka, eager to share some with me. At a high price, no doubt.

"Red, I am, ready to find the treasure. What a glorious day this will be! I thanked God in my prayers this morning knowing he will reward me for being a faithful servant," Sara was overjoyed and happy to be a Christian.

"Red, this day is part of God's plan. Here it is New Year's Eve, the day before we start our new life and a new year together," she lifted her opened arms towards the golden sun, dancing on the rear deck with joy in her heart.

"Sara, you may want to wait to see what God has planned. It might not be what you expect," I tried to caution her anticipation.

Chapter Eighteen

The Plan

WE TOOK A TAXI FROM the pier to the middle of the Cayman Islands, which is known as the Grand Cayman, a larger village then George Town. Most of the foreign banks were in George Town. However, I remembered the ninth bank of those many depository trips was the Grand Cayman National Bank.

In was about ten o'clock when we greeted the bank manager as he unlocked the main doors to the bank. I showed him my confidential bankbook with the private box number stamped on the cover. He guided us upstairs to a brick enclosed tomb where hundreds of locked boxes were on display, secured firmly into the walls.

I had a key and the official put his key into one of two locks, opening a large brass door enclosing a huge steel box. As I removed the box and put it on a nearby table; the official excused himself leaving the widow, Mrs. Darrel Emerson, alone with me to discover the treasure.

I reached in, found a large sealed brown envelope unaddressed and displayed it on the table next to the box.

Sara stated with a questionable tone, "No way could there be a million dollars in that packet."

I opened up the envelope and found a letter, opened it and read aloud...

"To whoever has discovered this bank box... You are reading this letter because you solved the puzzle I put into motion years ago; just in case I should die unexpectedly. For over ten years, I have spent millions of dollars trying to please my family and loved ones living in a facade. I was planning to retire and leave my deceitful life behind before my lies were uncovered. I'm hopeful I had an honorable funeral."

"The deposits made into eight offshore banks were part of an elaborate shell game to keep the money moving to avoid discovery. There is only one person who could have found this secret hiding place, my longtime confidant who expected nothing

from me, but served me to the end. I have rewarded
you. Thank you.

"God rest my soul in peace."

Darrel James Emerson

"Red, let me see that letter and the box," the charlatan woman forced her way to find only an empty container.

"That SOB, he lied to everyone, again. I have no idea who could be that confidential person. Maybe it's another one of his mistresses. Red, lets leave the islands in the morning before this chartered boat costs me all the money I have left from another failed marriage.

"Sara, I'll pay for the charter and the crew."

The End

Family Tree Series

This series of ten mystery novels will reveal how Sara Blake's actions and her decisions affect her children, their children and future generations.

The seeds of misdeeds and misconceptions poison the minds of the entire family including her ex-husband and her in-laws.

Over the past 50 years, some genetic family traits are celebrated; most are tainted with hate, vengeance, anger and greed. The world would be a better place if all seeds from the father and mother were good... but that is an unlikely story.

There is a lot of truth associated with this fictional family that spans four generations of faithful followers of the Christian teachings. Worshipping God does not guarantee anyone a life without pain and sorrow.

Honorable and resolute Christians struggle in life like everyone else. Their faith gives them hope for a better future; absolution from their transgressions with a promise for an everlasting life.

Red Herring witnesses first-hand, the sins and destruction of a family's integrity, their inheritance and their fundamental beliefs. Every family member will eventually lie, cheat, steal and kill in an effort to obtain their father's promise of wealth.

Escape from Freedom...Herring's first novel, encapsulates the Blake families' misdirected traditions and teaching that began generations ago.

Living in A Lie... Herring's next book soon to be published in the fall of 2014. There are many stories and examples of how undeserved wealth destroys Sara's second marriage in the course of her self-indulgence.

Scouting for Boys... this riveting story unveils the Harrison family's secrets that began in the 1960's. Curt, Sara's younger brother, was involved in Boys Scouts which changed the destiny of this entire Christian family.

The Legends of Lesvos... Herring followers will be intrigued to read how an ancient legend shapes Sara's life, her future and the future of the world. Christian scholars have been warning civilization for a thousand years, as Sara discovered in 1969 while attending Bible College.

The Internet Wife's Club... Redmond Herring actually began writing this book in 2001. Sara Blake creates a Website for abused women to help them get out of the relationship by enlisting others to help.

My Father's Seed... Herring watches and tells the reader how Morgan Blake takes control of his five children, their spouses and their children while preaching the gospel. This patriarch promises a better life while selling illegal drugs to high school students and college students.

Heirs in Judgment... The Blake family plots and executes a devious conspiracy to get control of a very wealthy businessman's assets and his money by recruiting the man's children who invade the dynasty.

Courtship of Deceit... In her quest to have great wealth, Sara centers her attention towards a wealthy widower whose wife mysteriously disappears in Cabos San Lucas, Mexico. Not only does she take advantage of the mogul's loneliness, she manipulates his vulnerability by taking control of his assets through marriage.

Harvesting the Sick... Sara Blake, with all her undeserved wealth, invests in a new medical insurance venture that provides free health insurance for the poor with a gruesome catch. Red Herring intervenes.

Comatose... Sara falls into a coma while at a hospital for a routine checkup. While she is out cold, her subconscious mind has a 'Come to Jesus meeting with GOD.' We can only pray for her soul.

"The Family Tree Series effectively connects Morgan Blake, Sara Harrison–Blake together, forever. These ten novels will be intriguing, foreboding and suspenseful illustrating how parents will change the lives of their children by making one bad decision," Redmond Herring

Redmond Herring Books
www.redmondherring.com

Escape from Freedom

By Redmond Herring

There is a lot of truth associated with this fictional family that spans three generations of faithful followers. Worshipping God and following the teaching of Christ, does not guarantee anyone a life without pain and sorrow.

Honorable and resolute Christians struggle in life like everyone else. Their faith gives them hope for a better future, absolution from their transgressions, and a promise for an everlasting life.

Like all mortal souls, the characters in this story have to survive the trials and tribulations of everyday life. Even a respected 'Man of God' with a Master's Degree in Divinity, must submit to the temptations of sin. His life, his family, his wealth and his inheritance are destroyed by a righteous indignation that repudiates the preacher's Sunday morning sermons.

Morgan Blake and his estranged wife must relent in their pursuit to surmount each other in their marriage dissolution, the custody of their five children and the division of marital assets.

As a faithful Baptist woman, she wanted to please her family by becoming a preacher's wife. How could she have known that her God-fearing husband would fall into temptation and destroy their marriage?

1 Timothy 6:10... "Some people, eager for money, have wandered from the faith and pierced themselves with many griefs."

After suffering under her pious husband's dominance for over 18 years, Sara kidnaps her five children leaving behind a wealthy dynasty.

This legally entangled mess harms everyone who wants the money. Some people go to jail. Some get divorced. Some lie and cheat, while others ask for absolution. The ramifications of the fall will cause pain and sorrow for generations.

The desire to get more money becomes the root of all kinds of evil including murder, arson and insurance fraud. The author witnesses the self-destruction of a religious zealot, a devoted wife and a faithful Christian family.

The desire for money, lots of money ruins the lives of those that seek unjust rewards.

Is wanting money evil? On the other hand, is it the seed of the father that encourages his heirs to covet their inheritance which is lost in the legal battles to keep their money?

All characters in this book should feel contrition for their sins and abjure for their sinful ways. Everyone involved (including this witness) were responsible for damaging the lives of two families... for generations to come.

There are many stories that branch out from one woman's life. The seeds of the father (and mother) have affected so many lives in so many ways.

My Family Tree Series reveals how the actions of the father (and the mother) affect future generations. The seeds of misdeeds and misconceptions poison the minds of all that follow.

These ideas and behaviors grew over time as each father passed on his seed for generations.

Redmond Herring Books

www.redmondherring.com